THE GENIUS BEASTS

By
FREDERIK POHL

Illustrated by
VIRGIL FINLAY

I0541531

ARMCHAIR FICTION
PO Box 4369, Medford, Oregon 97504

*For more information about Armchair Books and products, visit our
website at…*

www.armchairfiction.com

Or email us at…

armchairfiction@yahoo.com

WHISKED AWAY TO GANYMEDE...

For Nick and his friends it had started out as a simple sea voyage in a cabin cruiser. However, before long a huge ocean storm had turned their trip into a disaster; and when they ran afoul of a group of strange alien beings from outer space, disaster was turned into an amazing case of interplanetary kidnapping. What secret lay behind this extraordinary kidnapping and what was the intelligence behind it? Soon Nick and his comrades found themselves in the company of a strange woman on an even stranger world—Ganymede. And the woman, who seemed to know all the answers, was unable—or unwilling—to tell what she knew.

Surrounded by strange creatures, the three Earthmen found themselves in the unenviable position of finding out who, or what, had ordered their abduction, and most importantly…for what reason?

FOR A COMPLETE SECOND NOVEL, TURN TO PAGE 79

CAST OF CHARACTERS

NICK
Your typical American Joe from San Diego. He went for a boat ride—but ended up on Ganymede with a gorgeous alien babe!

DUNCAN
He was a good guy and a good pal to whom Nick would soon owe a lot—including his life.

TOMMY CLEELOCK
They say three's company, but when Tommy showed up, his two pals were overjoyed—especially since they thought he was dead!

"THE PINKIES"
Who were these strange aliens and what was their interest in Earth people—and what kind of meat did they actually eat…?

THE BOSS
A surly and detached warden, he was afraid of something—who was really the boss?

"HONEY"
This beautiful, mysterious female alien had all the answers Nick needed. Unfortunately she didn't speak a word of English!

THE KHREEN
These strange beings appeared to be simple alien beasts—but first impressions can sometime be wrong…

CHAPTER ONE

DUNCAN AND I were almost there before they took us out of the paralysis.

We had no way of telling how long we had been in the ship, unconscious and unable to move, but I was sure it had been a long, long time. I ached in every muscle, and when I moved I was sure I could actually hear myself creak.

The little pink man who called himself the Boss was watching when we woke up out of our dazed condition. "Don't make trouble," he advised us at once in his excited clipped tones. He carefully displayed a rod-like affair that I was willing to concede was a gun—though it might as well have been a pearl-handled back-scratcher. His English was amazingly good, considering that he was nowhere near human. He looked like a toad that was ambitious to become a leprechaun.

"Don't make trouble," he repeated, and: "It won't get you anywhere. Since you're awake I suppose you'll want to ask questions. Go ahead. I won't answer them, probably."

I looked at him and sat down on the hygienic, slightly resilient slab I'd been using for a bed. Questions? Sure I had questions, but what were they? Duncan got in first. "Why did you wake us up?" he asked with more objectivity than I owned. "Wouldn't it have been easier to keep us the way we were?"

"No. You were a damned nuisance. So was he," The last was accompanied by a webby, three-fingered gesture at me. I spoke up.

"What are you going to do with us?"

The pink imp leered. "You'll find out."

"When? And where are we going?"

"I won't tell you. I told you I probably wouldn't answer your questions. All you specimens ask the same things. It's none of your business." The toad-imp was frowning.

I shrugged and became practical. What he said didn't seem to matter very much, anyhow—possibly I was still under a hangover from the trance-like state we'd been in. "When do we eat?" I asked.

For the first time, the Boss stopped to think about a question. It occurred to me that he actually looked alarmed. He drew a thing like a lady's compact from the pouch he wore at his waist and flipped it open.

"Tomorrow," he announced with a glint of relief in his voice, after he had looked inside. "You get one meal before we land. Now you've asked enough questions. I won't answer any more. If there's anything you need, you can shout for it. Make sure you need it," he added sinisterly.

And he left, through a rather circular sort of door.

DUNCAN SAT down on his bed and looked at me. He said, "What do you think, Nick?"

I shrugged. I didn't know what to think. It was all pretty confusing.

Not so long before, life had been very simple. There was Duncan and there was I, and there was broad green water all around us and a little rubber life raft bouncing under us. There were no complications. All we had to do was reach land before we starved to death or overturned and drowned. Very simple.

As simple and natural as a Gulf Stream hurricane. When our cabin cruiser swamped and went down, I went down with it. By the grace of the good lord and the personal intercession of my patron saint, sometimes known as Santa Claus, I came up again close enough to Duncan and his life raft to clutch a thrown rope. The third member of our party, Tommy Cleelock, and the other life raft were nowhere in sight—which was true of anything more than twenty yards away, in that storm. We drifted all night. About noon the next day we saw a plane way off on the horizon, and a plume of smoke under it. There was no way of attracting their attention: we didn't even try. I like to think that they were looking for us, but as Duncan points out that was impossible; nobody would think of missing us for at least a week.

But a bit later we saw the loom of land.

We paddled toward it. We beached the life raft about an hour before dusk the second day, the hottest day of that or any year.

Everything was still and steaming hot. There was a malarial-looking jungle creeping down practically to the water line, but if there was any wild life in it, it was hiding. An unpleasantly muddy greenish stream was seeping along moldy ground, burying itself in the sand at the jungle's edge.

We didn't like the looks of it for drinking purposes, but thought it might be clearer near its source. So we struck into the heart of that deathly quiet jungle.

We found the end of our trip before we found the source of that brackish stream. Our life raft, for all I know, might still be on the beach, unless the tide took it away.

Though the little people more likely collapsed it and carried it off with them, the same time they took us; they were insufferably curious. I think that was the reason they had been promoted to the status of intelligence. With them, you see, evolution was not an abstract issue that two lawyers could debate in a courtroom. They knew about it, because they'd been through it themselves…

Anyway, we never found the source—because the little people found us first.

All the way up the stream we had the sensation of being followed. Finally, after looking furtively over our shoulders had showed us nothing, we just stood stock-still and waited.

It brought results.

There was a scrabbling in the underbrush and shrill, muted voices whispering musically about something. Then three little pink creatures—I've described the Boss; they all look about alike—hopped out of the jungle.

"Do not be afraid, men," one called to us. It wasn't what he said; it was sheer surprise at the looks of them that kept us from fighting them off, until it was too late. Before we collected ourselves we had been jabbed with tiny needles. There was a sharp pang, like a wasp's sting—

And, like a wasp's prey, we were paralyzed.

We stayed that way until they woke us up. Part of the time we were at least semi-conscious, because I remember one or two things in a hazy sort of way. The pink ones examining us, jabbing us with more needles, systematically disrobing us and then tossing the clothes back on us helter-skelter. I remember meeting the boss at one point—he was the English-speaking one—and being told that he gave the orders around there; we were to hop to it when he gave us any. He told us that himself.

And I remember being carried to a burned-out clearing where there rested a huge purplish torpedo of a ship—a rocket, in fact. We were dragged into it and put in a room, on a pair of soft, shock-absorbing pads. A pink one stuck his toad's head in the door a minute later to see that we were all right. And pretty soon thereafter there was a hell of a bang right below us and we felt sudden, sharp pressure.

The ship had taken off.

It seemed like a few days or weeks elapsed while we lay quiescent on those pads. Actually, I discovered later, it was a bit more than eighteen months!

I GOT around to answering Duncan's question with a question of my own.

"Where do you suppose we are?" I asked. "What goes on?"

Duncan grinned. He said. "That bespeaks immense faith in me, Nick. I'm sorry to let you down, but I don't know."

"Well, let's figure it out logically," I started, but Duncan halted me with a shake of the head. "There's no logic involved," he said. "The whole thing's screwy. I'm here, and I know I'm not dreaming, but I find it hard to believe all the same. Why don't we try the empirical method, Nick, and look around? Have you noticed..." He gestured. "...that the door's not closed?"

I stared at it. It was open all right, just a crack. I walked over to it, and was suddenly conscious of the fact that I had lost weight. I don't mean that I had lost fat; I hate euphemisms. I had the same mass as ever, but the acceleration of the ship, evidently, was less than one Earth gravity. By rough feel, I weighed perhaps a hundred pounds. A little less than two-thirds normal.

I stepped lightly to keep on the floor, conscious of a curious surge beneath me that was the throbbing of the rocket jets, and touched the door. It slid open all the way as soon as I laid my hand on it. I looked out, with Duncan breathing hotly on my shoulder.

"I can't see anything," Duncan said disappointedly. "Look, Nick, let's take a walk."

"You think we ought to? The Boss wouldn't like it."

Outside, the door was a corridor, metal-walled, floored with the same rubbery red stuff that was on the floor of our room. To our left it intersected with another corridor just like it, about five yards from us. To our right it ran a bit farther, then made a sharp bend; there were no other doors visible than the one we were leaning out of.

"I don't care what the Boss would like," Duncan said. "He didn't order us to stay here."

He broke off and listened. "Voices," he said excitedly. "Somebody's coming!"

I am a cautious man, so I grabbed the sleeve of Duncan's jacket and pulled him back into the room. I am also curious; I did not close the door.

I was glad that I hadn't closed it. The voices got louder—only it wasn't "voices." There was just one voice, a girl's. She was singing to herself quietly, the way you do when there's no one around to hear you. She wasn't singing in English, or in the kind of tonal music you hear over the radio. It was a liquid sort of language, totally incomprehensible, and the music flowed liquidly also. There were no breaks in it, no jump from note to note, but only a smooth flow. You could play music like that very well on a musical saw—or on the electronic gadget they call a theramin.

"Pretty voice," said Duncan, and I took a better grip on the sleeve of his gunner's tunic. "I hope she is as pretty—"

Then she passed the door, she and her...well, it looked like it was her pet; a great big shaggy dog that walked on its hind legs. It wore a thick metal collar around its ugly neck, and there was blankness and idiocy in its eyes. A hideous thing, all hairy and unpleasant, as big as a man.

She was not hideous. Neither was she human, I thought; probably it would have been too much to have expected a human girl there. But she was close enough...

I believe she was the most beautiful girl I ever saw. Tall and slender, but neatly and in fact sumptuously rounded where roundness is needful; vividly gorgeous of face. There was a height to her cheekbones and a quirk to the ends of her lips; a sort of hazy tilt to her eyes—Slavic, I thought she looked. I wonder how a Slav would have described her.

ALL THAT was human enough or superhuman. It was her hair that wasn't; it literally floated around her head, spider-silk thin and weightless. It was long and glistening, a pale pink corona that swirled and danced lazily as she walked. Quite a thing. Quite a damnably gorgeous thing, that any woman on Earth would have given half a lifetime to own.

I thought Duncan spoke to me. "Don't bother me," I said, keeping my eyes on the girl. "Tell me about it later."

"I didn't say anything," he protested. "I thought *you* spoke."

That disconcerted me enough to turn around and look at him. "Somebody spoke," I said; "somebody a long way off, maybe."

"That's what I heard," he nodded. Puzzled, I tried to reconstruct the feeling. It was a voice; I was sure, but I had no idea what it had been saying. But it didn't seem particularly important, and Duncan interrupted the thought.

"Hey," he said. "Front and center Nick. She's giving us the once-over."

She had stopped and turned around, and now she was looking at us, her lips still parted but no longer singing.

"Hello," said Duncan tentatively.

Her face grimaced involuntarily, as though she were repelled by the sound of his voice. But she controlled it and, after a moment, the frown vanished. Instead, her lips parted again and rich music came out, mocking music.

She was laughing at us.

"A fine reception we're getting, I must say," Duncan said disgustedly. "Lady, don't you know any better manners than that?"

Apparently she didn't because, still laughing, she turned around and left. We watched her pace slowly to the intersection, with that shaggy brute shambling along beside her, a silvery wire leash running from his collar to what looked like a similar collar around her own neck. She turned to the right and kept on walking, still singing. We listened to her voice die away. I wish I could make that melody into a symphony. It deserves it.

"Wow!" said Duncan, and he turned to look at me. I had never seen Duncan wide-eyed before; it was not an attractive sight. "I begin to like this place," he said. "I hope she's a permanent guest."

There was a squeal of high-pitched indignation from behind us. "Hey!" shouted a shrill voice. "What do you think you're doing?"

We spun around involuntarily. It was the Boss, racing down the corridor toward us with all boilers blazing and a deckhand sitting on the safety valve. "Get back in your cage!" he yelled. "You're not allowed out. Move!"

We moved, hurriedly. Greatly daring, Duncan said, "Who was that we just saw?"

The Boss' face took on a peculiar look that seemed almost like reverence. "The Khreen," he said.

"She's a pretty girl," Duncan commented. "Can we see her again?"

"Girl?" he asked scornfully. "Sure. She doesn't matter; she's just another specimen. You'll see plenty of her."

Duncan protested, "But you said she was..."

"Never mind what I said," the Boss interrupted, glaring at us from the doorway. "Now you stay here. If you want to get in trouble, just come out again. Big trouble, from me personally."

Duncan shrugged. "Why?" he asked reasonably. "We've been in here a long time. We're getting tired of it—and hungry, besides."

The Boss' glare faded a little and took on a sickly tinge. "You should complain," he said morosely, but didn't complete the thought. "I told you when you'd get fed. Tomorrow."

"Be seeing you then," I said.

The Boss' frog face split in a sardonic, unhappy grin. "That," he said, "is only too true." And he slid the door back, with a faint click we hadn't heard before. When Duncan tried it experimentally a little later, we found it was locked.

"Oh, well," he said. "We're not supposed to anyhow." He poked the resilient slab on his side of the room with a finger, then sprawled out on it.

"We might as well get some sleep," he said.

I followed his example, but I had a puzzlement in my mind that wanted settling. Before I fell asleep I said, "What do you suppose is biting on the Boss?"

Duncan, his back to me, shrugged. "No idea at all," he said. "Go to sleep. He'll probably tell you all about it, in his sour fashion, when we see him tomorrow."

CHAPTER TWO

But when we saw the Boss again he was in high spirits. "I like you," he said happily as soon as he was in the door. "Look—food."

He displayed two hunks of dripping meat, one in each webbed hand. He gave them to us and said, "Go ahead and eat; I'll watch you."

I took mine rather gingerly and gave it a thorough inspection. It had not been cooked, apparently, but it was quite warm. I sniffed it and liked what I smelled, so I took a nibble.

I've tasted worse. It was odd, but edible. If you fed a pig on herring for a couple of months before slaughtering him, then smoked the hams in the fumes of Chinese incense, it might taste like that. It wasn't unbearably bad, once you got used to it.

Finding the Boss in a good humor was so unexpected that we didn't take advantage of it for a while. When I'd finished gnawing on my chunk of meat I broke the conversational ice. "Why wouldn't you let us look out the door yesterday?" I asked tentatively. "Was it that girl? Is she taboo or something?"

He grinned, but amiably. "I won't tell you. Don't you know that I'll tell you hardly anything?"

"I'm beginning to find out," I agreed, quite sincerely.

His face clouded as though I had hurt his feelings. He said, "I'll tell you one thing, because I like you. Today we

land. This is the end of our voyage—and I've finished another trip alive!"

I gaped at him. He was positively beamish over his
triumph of survival, grinning to himself like a moonstruck
leprechaun. "Shall I show you something?" he whispered
conspiratorially. "Something you'd like to see? I oughtn't
to do it, but it doesn't matter. And I like you. Shall I show
you?"

"Sure," said Duncan. I nodded eagerly.

"All right," said the Boss. He opened the door, stepped
out into the corridor. "Come on," he said.

We followed him, Duncan and I. We turned to the
right at the door, followed along the corridor to where it
made its sharp bend to the left, then walked a few paces
along the new corridor. He stopped before a door and
craned his thick neck anxiously to look at us.

"Do you know why I like you?" he asked suddenly. "It
is not because of anything you did. You are rather
loathsome to me, you know. Oh, it's not your fault; all of
you specimens are basically revolting, when you come right
down to it. You can't help it... I like you," he said, "because you do not eat very much."

He grinned happily. "You don't understand?" he said in
high good humor. "Of course you don't; you weren't
expected to. Now, we will go in here. Conduct yourselves
well, because I will kill you if you get me in trouble. I
would have no compunctions. I don't like you *very* well."

With a grand gesture he flung the door open and
motioned us in.

WE FOUND ourselves in a large room. It was filled
with some of the most fantastic hunks of gadgetry you'll

see in a month of Whitsuntides. "Jeepers," said Duncan, and it expressed my feelings perfectly.

There were machines in the room…but such machines as I had never come across before. Little ones and big ones; square ones and one that seemed to be made out of odds and ends of runny tar and crepe paper—shapeless.

One of the gadgets dominated the entire thirty-foot room. It would have dominated any room. It was quite sensational.

There was a shallow tank of an orange liquid, rectangular, with a fountain coming up out of the middle. It was decorative—a curious flashing jet of brilliant orange—but its function was not merely decoration. For there was a small group standing in the pool, two or three pinkies, a couple of the dog-beasts, and the girl.

"What a way to take a shower," Duncan breathed over my shoulder.

That's what it looked like. From the falling orange spray, from the jet of the fountain itself, from the surface of the pool, droplets of what looked like pure radiant energy were forming, drifting about and dropping back to the pool. Fat orange sparks, that weren't electricity because they didn't crackle or spit, just collected and floated lazily around and down. Where they were drifting the thickest, there stood the pinkies and their companions, standing there with eyes closed and expressions of seraphic rapture on their faces, letting the sparks, or whatever, soak into them.

I heard the Boss puffing contentedly beside me. "What is it?" I asked him. "What are they doing?"

It was a stupid question, of course, because I knew what his answer would be. "I won't tell you," he said delightedly. "Anyway, that's not what I brought you here to see. I wanted— Hey! Come back!"

He was talking to Duncan's back. Duncan's front, followed by the rest of Duncan, was heading purposefully toward the tank, and the girl.

The Boss shrieked in pure rage and jumped for Duncan. He leaped on his back, dragging him back toward me. I stood paralyzed. Duncan grunted. "What—what's the matter," half choked by the Boss' throttling arm.

"Animal! Beast! I told you to obey orders! It is death for you if you touch the life-waters!" He released Duncan and jumped back, panting heavily, his hand close to the paralysis needle he carried in his belt.

Duncan shrugged. "All right," he said; "I just wanted to talk to the girl."

"Talk! Hah! You couldn't understand her. You think our people bother to learn your stupid tongue?"

"You did," Duncan pointed out. "Besides, you said she was a specimen too. From Earth, like us, I take it?"

The Boss snorted. Aggrievedly he said, "Never mind about her. This is what I get for being good to you. Animals!"

"Sorry," said Duncan in resignation. "Lead on, Boss."

He scowled blackly, then jerked his thumb to the far corner of the room. "Over there," he said bitterly.

In the corner was another door. We marched over to it—or glided might be a better word, because our Earth-trained strides gave us an odd bounce at every step in the light drag. The Boss flung the door open.

"Look inside," he ordered, his tone becoming calmer.

We looked. The sparks from the tank were drifting about and, though they weren't very dense, it was strangely hard to see through an atmosphere that was all cluttered up with fat, luminescent hunks of orangeness. Where they were thickest it was like trying to look down into the waters off Bermuda on a muggy August night when a boat has just stirred up the plankton.

But I looked, and I saw, finally, who it was that was sitting there, staring at me with a curiously angry expression on his face. I might not have recognized him at first, but he said, "Hi-ya, palsies," and that clinched it. It was Tommy Cleelock, raised from the dead.

"BUT HE WAS drowned," Duncan objected. I shook my head.

"Not Tommy," I told him. "He'll never drown. Born to hang."

Cleelock got up and walked over to us. "So they got you too," he observed, and I saw that he was white-lipped. His voice was taut, too, though his words were easy enough.

"Surprised to see us, Tommy?" I asked inanely. "Well, we're surprised—"

"Nah," he said; "they told me you were alive. Didn't know you were on this ship, but I had a pretty good idea you might be."

"Oh," I said. There was a brief silence. Then Duncan said: "Well, *I'm* surprised. What are *you* doing here?"

"Same thing you are," he told us. "How do you like being a human sacrifice?"

"Human sacrifice?"

Tommy grinned mirthlessly, jerked a thumb at the Boss. "Ask him?"

The Boss frowned. "You are making trouble," he accused. "You specimens will not be hurt; you are wanted only for research."

"Sure, research. Like vivisection, for instance."

The Boss tossed his head and didn't deign to answer.

"Look," I said earnestly to Tommy, "tell me more about this. I want to know what you're talking about."

"Oh, it's nothing," Tommy said morosely. "Just don't count on ever seeing home again, that's all. We're going to Ganymede."

"Ganymede? What's Ganymede?"

"Ganymede," Tommy explained, "is one of the moons of Jupiter. The planet. That's where we're going."

"Oh," I said. I will say for myself that I took that calmly enough—after all, the signs had been pointed straight to something of the sort. "Uh—why Ganymede?" I asked.

"Because that's where he comes from," Tommy pointed again to the Boss.

The Boss nodded, grinning widely. "Naturally. I come from Ganymede," he said superiorly. "You didn't think Mars, did you? You thought maybe people lived on Mars, that dry old place? Ho-ho-ho! Stupid!"

"All right," I said pacifically. "Anyway, what I'm interested in is—what happens to us when we get there?"

Tommy said earnestly, "If I knew the answer to that, I'd sell you the information at a million dollars a word. That character..." He pointed again at the Boss. "...gives double talk, exclusively."

"You'll find out," the Boss said cryptically. He yawned, showing a mouth full of randomly spaced teeth. "I leave you for a while," he announced, and closed the door from outside. Apparently he was going over to chat with his spark-bathing friends.

Tommy shook his head mournfully. "To think I taught him everything he knows," he observed. "Gratitude!"

"What did you teach him?" I asked.

"Everything!" He leaned back against a bulkhead and looked sad. "I lost you, see, during the storm. I see Duncan go off with the stern life raft, and I drag the other one out of the cabin. I get it into the drink and fall in with it, and the next thing I see of anything but water, I'm drifting onto this island. I go ashore and wander around. Everything goes fine, until all of a sudden I see things moving. It's these little pink devils. One of them sneaks up on me, and stabs me when I'm not looking, and—zap, I'm out like a light." He glared at me.

"I didn't do it," I protested hastily. "What then?"

"Well—" he scratched his head. "Then come things I don't understand. I wake up, and I'm in this thing, which according to the Boss is a rocket ship. Only he doesn't tell me this at that time, because at that time he doesn't speak any English. So I teach it to him."

"You do—I mean, you did?" I thought it over. "We've been gone longer than I thought, maybe. His grammar stinks, but it's no worse than yours. Must have taken him months to learn it."

TOMMY shook his head. "Don't interrupt," he said. "First, you're right; we've been gone longer than you thought. Don't know how long, but it's months—the Boss told me. Second, it didn't take him long to learn English. All I did was talk. He caught on like a knitted sweater in a barbed-wire fence. He sat there in my cell, with his pet baboon scratching fleas next to him, watching me until I got nervous. Then he began pointing to things. I'm no dope; I got the idea Quick. I told him the names of everything in sight, and acted out a couple of simple verbs, and by and by all I had to do was answer his questions. Amazing."

"How long did it take?" I asked curiously.

"You won't believe me."

"How long?"

He sighed. "Two days."

I straightened up and gave him the eye. "Cleelock," I said, "you're a cockeyed liar."

He shrugged without resentment. "I told you," he reminded me. "I wouldn't have believed it either. But the little son never forgot a thing. It was terrific. I guess he doesn't believe in sleep, or something—I passed out twice the first day, still talking, before he would believe that I had to get a little rest. Yammer, yammer, yammer. I never heard so much talking in my life. We talked about everything under the sun," He shook his head. "He asked more questions than the Internal Revenue bureau. I—I had an idea somebody was helping him with his homework, if you get what I mean. Suggesting questions to him, helping him figure out the answers. But there wasn't anybody else in the room."

"Did he tell you anything about what they plan to do with us?"

"A couple of things. He said we were going to Ganymede, and, no, I'd never go back. He said something that sounded very unpleasant about surgical tests—then he clammed up." A troubled look came into Cleelock's eyes. Slowly he said, "One funny thing he told me—I don't get it, exactly. I was describing a dog to him. He got all excited, then he decided that *he* was a dog."

"Huh," I said. "Maybe he meant he was an animal."

"No, I don't think so—at least, not exactly. Later on I began on class nouns. He let 'animal' go by without an objection, but when I came to 'pet', he decided he was one of those. You know what that means?"

I thought it over. "Pet," I said. You mean he's just a domestic animal?"

Cleelock spread his palms. "You know as much as I do," he said. "But that's the impression I got—except that, if they don't run their planet, who does?"

Duncan, with his jaw hanging, snapped it shut and nodded wisely. "The girl," he said.

I said, "No—not according to the Boss. Remember? He said she was a specimen like us."

Cleelock brushed me off. "Girl?" he asked. "What girl?"

"Why, the red-head in the corridor. The slick-chick soprano."

But Tommy hadn't seen the girl at all. When we finished telling him about her he was all excited. "This might not be so bad, hey?" he said, his eyes glittering. "She sounds like a knockout."

Before I could think of a good squelching remark the Boss came back. "Visit's over," he said, staring in at us through the door. "We go back to your cage."

Tommy glared at him. "I could dislike you," he said. Then, significantly, "I'm getting a little hungry, by the way."

The Boss flinched. "You are not," he protested feebly; "you just ate."

I asked, "What's the gag?"

"Don't you know?" Cleelock laughed in somber glee. "It's the only thing we've got on these characters. Have you eaten yet?"

"Why, sure."

"What did you have?"

I was puzzled. "Some kind of meat; it was raw, but it tasted all right."

Cleelock nodded superiorly. "Know what it was?" he asked.

"No." I looked curiously at the Boss, who seemed acutely unhappy. Then I got it, and gasped. "You mean that meat—"

"Yep," said Tommy. "What you ate was a piece of pink devil. It's the only kind of food they carry."

CHAPTER THREE

I GAVE up eating for the rest of the trip. Fortunately, that was only a matter of a few hours, but the way I felt I never wanted to eat again anyhow. The Boss wasn't exactly my own race, but he spoke English and seemed intelligent…and cannibalism had never appealed to me.

Duncan and I talked it over rather unhappily, and came to no important conclusion. It seemed so revoltingly impossible—but the Boss hadn't denied it.

We let it go and laid back on our slabs to brood over the whole thing. A couple hours after we left Tommy Cleelock the Boss came into our cubbyhole and ordered us to stay on the slabs. Then he departed, and presently we felt the ship begin to slam around as though it were being jockeyed in for a landing—which, obviously, it was. There was one final jolt, and a bump, and the throbbing of the engines died.

The Boss and one of his pink helpers trotted in. They prodded us down the corridor to the exit hatch, picking up Tommy Cleelock on the way.

We came out onto a landscape with a lavender sky.

"So this is Ganymede," Duncan breathed. "Flat, isn't it?"

I agreed with him. There wasn't a mountain in sight. Maybe time and erosion did it—Ganymede, I found out later, is an ancient, ancient world—or maybe it was that way to begin with. But the only thing that broke the level of the horizon was a group of immense spires maybe fifteen miles away.

Duncan pointed to it. He said, "That looks like a pretty big city. Bigger than New York even, maybe."

"Maybe," said Cleelock derisively. "Those buildings are a good mile high."

"Come on, come on," the Boss said in his peevish, high-pitched voice. "Don't keep us waiting." I looked behind us, and the Boss had been joined by a couple more pinkies, convoying the gorgeous girl and her beast. A couple more pinkies were trotting around the corridors on what seemed to be urgent errands, but I didn't bother to watch them. I was looking at the girl.

I took a good look at her, and by the fact that Cleelock was breathing hard I could tell that he was doing the same. Nearby and in daylight, she was prettier than I had imagined. I could see, though, that she was not the human being I'd taken her for. What the Boss said about her being a specimen like us crossed my mind, but I brushed it aside. Like us she was not. Her whole build was too delicate, too slight for humanity and the pinkish aurelle that hung about her head was much too fine to be the hair of a human.

"I said come *on*," snapped the Boss, and nudged us toward a thing on wheels. It was more like a canoe than a car, but we got in, all of us, and the pinky who sat in front fiddled with some push-buttons and the car began to move. It was headed off at a right angle from the direction of the city, and I was about to say something about it, when we rounded the stern of the purple rocket. I saw another city spread before us.

But it wasn't much of a city.

I took a quick look at the one behind us for comparison. There was no comparison. When the one on the horizon was tall and slender, this one was squat and ugly. The one was a spiry fairyland of towers, the other an alphabet-block collection of cubes.

"Wouldn't you know it?" murmured Cleelock. "We end up in a Ganymedan slum."

"Shut up," the Boss said petulantly. I stole a look at him. His unpredictable mood had changed again; where a couple of hours before he had been almost affable, now he was his customary surly self.

THE CAR skidded as the driver twirled a little rod, and came round in an arc to head for the nearest of the cubes. I could see at close range, that the buildings hadn't even windows to recommend them—nothing but a blank facade of what looked like cheap stucco.

"Maybe they'll let us live in the rocket," Duncan suggested. "This place doesn't look like home to me."

The car skidded to a stop before our destined cube and, on orders from the Boss, we hopped out and walked inside. We all three had to bend over to enter, because the frame of the door was cut for someone about five feet four or less. Inside, the ceilings were a uniform six feet above the floor, a fact that I deduced from the angle at which six-foot-one Tommy Cleelock's head was bent.

We were assailed by a loud metallic clanging. "What the devil," Cleelock said. "What's that noise?"

We listened. "Air pumps, maybe?" I guessed. It was a rhythmic clash, and it sounded like air pumps if it sounded Eke anything at all. But so loud!

"Fine," said Duncan in complete disgust. "What do you make of that? These people build terrific rocket ships, but when it comes to a simple thing like an air-conditioning system they fall flat on their faces. I never heard so much noise."

"Maybe they like noise," I guessed; "maybe they don't care."

Before we could carry the conversation any farther the witch-girl interrupted. Staring at us, she trilled something musical—not to us, but almost as though she were just lightheartedly bursting into song. But there was an answer from the Boss. He ripped off a brief burst of melody—I thought that, compared to her, he was a little flat—and then scowled at me.

"Do you specimens need to sleep now?" he asked gruffly.

I looked at the others, who seemed rested enough. I said, "No."

"How about eating?"

"Well—" I hesitated over the answer. "If it's true about eating *you*—"

He winced. "That was only on the ship," he said hastily. "Here we have other things—plants, or something. Whatever you specimens usually eat."

"That would be fine," I said.

WE ATE pale blue, thick-stemmed ferns. They were peppery, but the Boss snapped pettishly that they were all right. "Better than you deserve," he added. "Anyway, you won't really have to worry about eating much longer, probably—" a remark which I considered in notoriously bad taste.

Duncan chopped off a fern stem with a dull flat knife they had given us and stared at the girl. She was standing near us, day-dreaming. Apparently she didn't bother to eat any more than the rest of this nightmare bunch but Duncan tried offering her a piece of fern. It got him but nowhere...she looked through, over and beyond him, but never eye to eye. She wasn't avoiding him deliberately; he just plain didn't make any impression.

"Where's her two-legged sheepdog?" Duncan asked suddenly. Reminded, I looked around, but the animal wasn't in the room.

Cleelock volunteered, "The Boss took it out for a walk. Didn't you see? The gal had a collar around her neck, attached to the leash. She took it off, and the Boss put it on, and the two of them walked out, him and the beast." He chuckled. "That's a terrific arrangement they have," he commented. "Both the Boss and the dog wear collars when they go out walking—you can hardly tell which is master and which is dog."

When the Boss came back, he had the animal with him sure enough, and both wore the flat silvery collars.

The Boss said, in a tone that was new and surprising simply because it was tranquil. "Come along with us, all three of you." He looked at the girl and a ripple of music came from his batrachian lips. She trilled a reply, showing interest in the proceedings for the first time, and he turned and led us out of the room.

In the hall, the raucous clangor of the air pumps was twice as bad as in the room where we had been fed. We faced it with gritted teeth and allowed ourselves to be conducted to what looked to be an elevator. We all got in, the Boss pushed a button and closed the door; a second's wait and the door opened.

"Well," said Cleelock. "Things are looking up. I like their no-jar elevators."

I nodded. After their unpleasantly inefficient air-conditioning, this latest taste of Ganymedan technology had been a pleasant surprise. There hadn't been a hint of jolting or motion, yet now we were looking out on another corridor, this one broad and well lighted.

The Boss led the way. He took us to a large room that looked like, and turned out to be, a surgery.

"Hey," said Cleelock in an alarmed tone. "Boss, what are you planning to de here?"

"Test you," the Boss said. "Sit down."

"Test us for what?"

The Boss shrugged—or tried to shrug; his shoulders were of about the same dimensions as his neck, and all he achieved was a sort of twitch. "To see what we can do with you, of course," he said. He pointed to the redhead. "For instance, we might give you the treatment we gave her."

I looked at the girl. Whatever the "treatment" was, she didn't seem in terribly bad shape. Extra *good* shape, in fact, I would have said. But still—

"What's the treatment like?" I asked. "What did you do to her? Was she like us once?"

"Like you? No. She was female. And much smaller."

"But what did you do to her?" I begged.

PLACIDLY the Boss waved a hand. "What we did to her," he said serenely, "was what was done once to all of us. She came from your dirty little planet, and was captured as a specimen. She was very tiny. There were others with her." He looked us over speculatively. "About the size of you, they were," he said. "They died."

"Awk," I said involuntarily. I covered up with a question. "Do you have many specimens from our planet?" I asked.

"No. Just you three. And her."

"What did—I mean, what did the others die of?"

He smiled benignly. "Various things," he said.

"Now, look, Boss—" Cleelock started to get up and remonstrate. The Boss scowled.

"Sit down!" he said, and Cleelock sat down. More calmly, the Boss went on, "I will tell you a story to quiet your nerves. It begins here on Ganymede, just under a million of your years ago."

"I don't want a story," Cleelock protested. "I want—"

"I don't care what you want," the Boss said mildly but finally. "This story is about solitary confinement. Not one man in solitary confinement, though. A whole race."

Cleelock said, "How can a race be solitary, Boss?"

The Boss glared. "All right," he said angrily, "I won't tell you; I was against it anyhow."

Cleelock pulled in his horns. "Wait a minute, Boss. Let's—let's hear the story. Before you—test us, I mean."

The Boss shook his head. He pointed to the door. "Too late," he said ominously. "The examiners are ready."

We looked apprehensively at the door.

Three pinkies were coming in, each with a shaggy beast on a leash to keep him company. The foremost of them was struggling under a clumsy object that looked a little like an electric chair. He set it down, fussed with some gadgets on the back of it and looked at me expectantly. He sang a little song of invitation.

"All right," said the Boss—but to my relief, he was talking to Cleelock instead of me. "Sit down."

Cleelock dazedly stumbled over to the chair and sat, net with any appearance of comfort.

The Boss called something musical; the pinky by the chair touched something among the gadgets; there was a quick crackle of energy.

Cleelock's body became completely transparent. "Hey!" he squawked. "What's going on?"

"Oh, Tommy," I said. "You look funny. I can see right through you."

"Well, *I* can't see a thing." He was peering frantically around the room, his eyes like a blind man's. "Everything's all out of focus, like. What *is* this?"

"Your cornea doesn't refract," I started to say learnedly—but by the time I got the words out it didn't matter. The pinkies had conferred briefly in musical sounds, and the sound of energy died. Cleelock's body once more became opaque, and his naked skeleton was clothed with flesh.

"Take it away," he moaned. "I'll be good."

The Boss was gesturing to me and, there being no help for it, I took my place in the hot seat. When the juice came on it didn't fry me as I had expected. In fact there was no sensation at all, except the peculiar inability to focus my vision that had troubled Cleelock. Everything ran lumpily together, and nothing looked like anything at all. Involuntarily I closed my eyes to shut out the sight. That was a gross error. It's bad enough seeing chaos with the eyes open. When your eyelids have become transparent, and you can feel them pressed tightly shut, and still you see a maelstrom of light and color, then it is bad.

But it didn't last. A few seconds and I was replaced by Duncan. And a few more seconds and we were all through.

The Boss was talking things over with the three other pinkies. Then he turned to us, his face registering dissatisfaction.

"How'd we come out, Boss?" I asked hopefully.

"Hah," he said darkly. "No good."

"No good?"

"No. You are too old; we cannot give you the treatment. That means only one thing," he added, scowling darkly. "There must be purification!" And he pointed to the door with a theatrical gesture.

WE TROOPED out as he directed, back to the elevator. Inside he pressed another of the buttons, and the door closed and opened as before. "What do you make of this 'purification' business?" whispered Cleelock. "Sounds bad to me."

But before I could answer the door was open again, and bright sunlight was streaming in.

We looked out onto what seemed to be a roof garden. I gathered, from our position about forty feet from the edge of it, that it was no small roof, either. To judge by the way the horizon looked we were a good thousand feet in the air.

We were standing on a path made of translucent, reddish stone. All about us grew bushes and trees.

"Come along," said the Boss, mildly enough, and pointed to a pond. We walked ahead of him, and I stared down into it.

Whatever it was, it wasn't water. It was the same stuff I had seen in the fountain back on the ship—a livid orange liquid with all the appearance of fire. A still, limpid flame, so vivid that I expected heat and was surprised when there was none.

"Whaddya know," exclaimed Cleelock. "A fishpond of Martinis!"

The Boss marched up beside us and, benignly resting a hand on the sloping shoulder of his faithful beast, addressed us.

"Jump in," he said.

"What?"

Pettishly, "Jump in!"

Cleelock said determinedly, "No. Look, Boss, that stuff's dangerous. How do we know what it is? Maybe it's acid."

The little ridges of muscle where the Boss' eyebrows should have been went up. "You refuse to jump?" he asked incredulously.

"Well, yes." Cleelock stood his ground.

The Boss turned to me. "Jump in!"

"I'd—I'd rather not."

And Duncan chimed in, "Me too. I don't see the sense in it."

The girl, who had been watching us wide-eyed, sang something questioning and rapid to the Boss, who gave her a quick arpeggio in return. To us he said, "You don't have any choice, you specimens; you must go in the pool. It is for the purification. Besides, I tell you to!"

"Huh-uh." Cleelock shook his head vigorously, Duncan and I backing him up. "Be reasonable, Boss. That stuff looks kind of deadly."

I expected the Boss to tear into a tantrum but he merely glowered indecisively for a moment, then ripped off a many-noted bugle call in the general direction of the bushes. There was a moment of waiting, then half a dozen pinkies appeared. The Boss, scowling at us, sang them a catchy little air that boded us no good.

Like football players getting ready for a line back, they formed a wedge and advanced on us, edging us closer to the pool.

"Wait a minute," Duncan begged. "Look, Boss, we're the specimens you like. Remember? We don't eat much."

"In the pool," snarled the Boss. "Jump!"

The three of us were huddled together, giving ground slowly and unwillingly. Cleelock, next to me, swore under his breath. "Okay. Nick," he whispered. "He's asking for it. When I jump for the Boss, you grab the girl. Duncan—you take one of the others. Anyone. Got it?"

"Huh?" I asked stupidly, but I felt his hand prodding something into mind. It was flat and coldly metallic, and I found out—the hard way—that it had a sharp edge. It was one of the knives they'd given us to eat with! Cleelock had been smarter than either Duncan or me—he'd thought to snatch the knives for a future emergency!

"Jump!" the Boss said coldly again, and the other pinkies came on toward us. We retreated until there was nothing behind us but pool. Then—

"Now!" roared Cleelock, and sprang for the Boss. A split second behind him, I grabbed the girl, held the knife to her flimsily covered torso. She shrieked a terrified coloratura aria, the Boss squawked in surprise and Cleelock bellowed: "Now we'll see who's running things! Boss, call off your dogs—or we'll puncture your gizzard!"

THE PINKIES froze in consternation. For a moment it looked as though we had the situation well under control, but it didn't last. The Boss frothed:

"You foolish men! There are too many of us—you must go in the pool!" And he shrieked something in their polytonal tongue, and the other pinkies came on.

Cleelock wavered and Duncan and I watched him for our cue. Then he cursed furiously and threw down his knife. "Hit that line!" he bellowed, and lunged into the knot of pinkies.

Duncan and I piled into them after him. It could have been slaughter if we had used the knives, but we didn't have to. Their childlike, light-gravity bodies were like straws in our way.

We hurled them aside, boiled through and bounded for the elevator cage, Cleelock showing the way. Surprise and the simple business of picking themselves up from where we'd thrown them kept the pinkies a reasonable distance behind us, and Cleelock had time to fumble around with the buttons. He chose one at random, poked it...

It worked! The door slid shut. There was a brief pause; it opened again. No jolt, no lurch, no jar...but we were no longer on the roof. We were looking out into a pitch-black corridor.

Cleelock poked his head out tentatively. Nothing happened; we all stepped out, looked up and down. Utter blackness, not a fleck of light anywhere, except what came from the elevator itself.

"Now what?" whispered Duncan.

"It beats me," I said. "Maybe this is the cellar." The car was as dark as your alimentary canal. There was nothing to show that anyone had ever been there—in fact, I realized suddenly, there wasn't even the racket of their clashing air-conditioning pumps.

"Spooky," I whispered. "Let's go someplace else."

Well, it was the wrong thing to do, on the face of it. The darker and the more deserted, the better a place was for our purposes. But there was something so lonesome and desolate about that corridor that we didn't stop to.

think things over. We piled back into the car and turned to Cleelock, and Cleelock turned to the board of buttons. He reached up for the handiest one. The door slid closed, and we braced ourselves to see what floor we'd land on this time. The door opened.

Sunlight poured in.

"Holy heaven!" gasped Cleelock. "We're back on the roof!"

One glance convinced me—it was a roof, all right. "Don't just stand there," I begged. "Get us out of here before the pinkies realize we're back!"

Cleelock nodded quickly and stretched out his hand. Just as his finger was settling on a button Duncan stopped him with a quick, incredulous gesture. "Wait a minute," he said. "Take a look around. This isn't the same roof!"

THAT GAVE us pause to think. I gaped out onto the roof, and what Duncan said was incontrovertibly the truth.

I vividly remembered the other roof. There had been a sort of glassy-pavemented path, and well-kept trees and bushes, and the pond. And most of all, there had been the pinkies. Here there were none of those things. Here there were only a few patches of scraggly grass. And the edge of the roof was much nearer, because this roof was not very large.

Cleelock spat angrily. "Characters," he said. "They build houses with two roofs."

Duncan said wonderingly, "That other roof—could we have been mistaken? Was it just a terrace, maybe? A gallery sticking out from one of the lower floors?"

Cleelock snorted. "And the rest of the building invisible, huh? Did you see any higher stories—or do you see any now?"

"Well, no. But, Tommy—"

"But Tommy nothing! Terrace, the man says. How could it be a terrace?"

"All right, Steinmetz. What was it? *Two* roofs, like you said?"

Cleelock's truculence puffed away. "Search me," he said weakly; "all I know is, I am not happy."

I could see the other buildings about us. They were tall towers and spires, not like the cubes I remembered seeing as we approached the city. Then I had an idea. I said, "Let's settle the argument. If it was a terrace, we'll be able to see it over the side of the roof. Why not take a look?"

"Why not?" echoed Duncan. The three of us headed for the edge…cautiously, because the architect of this edifice had neglected to include a guardrail in his plans. We peered down, afflicted with severe vertigo.

No terrace. In fact, nothing at all. Nothing but a straight, sheer breathtaking drop that looked to be a thousand light-years, and must in fact have been at least a mile.

The three of us recoiled from that murderous brink and stood still yards away, quieting our shattered nerves. "What a dope," moaned Cleelock. "You still want to look for that terrace? Maybe it's on the other side."

"No," said Duncan, and there was a definite note of strain in his voice. "No," said Duncan, and there was a definite note of strain in his voice. "No, it's not on the other side."

I looked at him curiously. "How do you know?"

"Take a look." He waved weakly off into space. "Look beyond that pinkish sort of tower over to the right. Way off on the horizon—see it?"

I peered out over the edge of the room. There was a strong breeze blowing, and it made my eyes water. I had difficulty in focusing, and while I was squinting Cleelock spotted it. "You mean—oh, yeah. It's another city. Looks all cubical, like this one."

"No," said Duncan. "*Not* like this one. Do you recognize that purple thing between the city and us?"

"Why, no. That is, it does look a little familiar—ulp!"

Cleelock abruptly ran out of words, and just about that time I saw what they were talking about.

There was a cubical kind of city. Before it, made tiny by the distance but still recognizable, was a purple torpedo of a rocket ship. The very rocket in fact, in which we had come.

"But that's impossible," I said reasonably. "That's the city we're *in.*"

CHAPTER FOUR

We stood gaping at that city for quite a while before we could believe it; and then we weren't sure. It was a good fifteen miles from us. Fifteen miles that we had covered apparently, in the time it took for the elevator door to open and shut. But how?

Cleelock said tentatively, "That elevator must not have been an elevator, I guess."

"Then what was it?"

He shrugged. "I don't know what you'd call it. Maybe a rocket, or a subway, or something; whatever it is, it sure got us from there to here in a hurry."

Duncan said practically, "Well, let's not worry about it. The important thing is…what are we going to do? As I see it we're in a pretty bad jam, and no relief in sight. We're stuck on Ganymede. We've got nothing to eat, no weapons, no friends. The only people we know on the whole planet want to dunk us in what looks like a sulfuric acid swimming pool."

I said, "We still have our knives; at least. I have mine. Maybe we could catch one of the pinkies, and force him to take us to the rocket, and then—"

Cleelock snorted. "And then *what?* I left my pilot's license in my other suit."

"That's right," Duncan chimed in. "We can't fly a rocket. Even if we could, there's something else. What's all this talk about *forcing* a pinky to do anything? We tried that, remember? And look what happened?"

"Well, I guess you're right," I admitted. "They don't seem to mind the idea of death. The whole thing is screwy," I pondered on the matter for a second. "Maybe it was a bluff," I suggested. "I wondered if the Boss actually thought we would kill him, back there on the other roof. Maybe he thought we were bluffing, and ran a counter-bluff of his own, and it worked."

"I think not," Duncan said meditatively. "He believed us all right. You know, Tommy, the more I think about it, the more I'm struck by something you told us."

Cleelock said, "And what was that?"

"You said the Boss claimed to be a dog. Well—maybe he is."

I said doubtfully, "We've been over this once before. You had the idea that it meant the pinkies weren't the ruling race on this planet—that they were just domestic animals of some kind. But if it isn't them, who is it? Surely we'd expect to see the ruling race of a planet. It can't be the girl—the Boss said she was just a specimen like us, and only one of her at that."

Duncan spread his hands. "I give up," he announced resignedly. "It just doesn't add up. Things check to a certain point. The pinkies think of themselves as pets; they are willing to be killed in order to do their jobs—they even offer themselves as food for us. But right there the proposition collapses. If they don't run this planet, who does?"

"The redhead's pet monster, maybe," Cleelock suggested, and we all laughed grimly.

Duncan stared around us. He said. "We haven't solved the main question. What do we do?"

There was a silence. Then Cleelock said, "I know one thing; we can't just let things ride—we'd starve to death. How about trying out Nick's suggestion?"

"You mean forcing one of the pinkies to take us to the ship?" I asked.

"No. Not one of the pinkies—the girl." He ran an irate hand through his hair. "I don't care what the Boss says—if his race doesn't rule this planet, the girl's must. He can't pass her off as human. You know what she looked like. Pretty, yes. Human—good Lord, no—not with that hair. But believe me—human or not, there never was a woman that I couldn't order around. Let me handle her—that's all I ask."

Duncan looked at me doubtfully. I said, "What can we lose?"

"All right." He nodded, and turned back to the well, let's keep calling it an elevator.

The door of the car was closed. Cleelock tore his hair. "Wouldn't you know it?" he moaned. "Say! Does that mean somebody's using the thing—somebody that might be chasing us with it?"

"Probably," Duncan said in a flat tone. And the expression of despair on his face added the words: *And if so, what can we do about it?*

Cleelock closed his eyes. "Well," he said, and his voice was like a prayer, "there must be some way to open that door. We'd better find it. And when we do, the plan still goes."

But it didn't go, really, because we couldn't open the door.

We hunted high and low on the blank face of it, and found—nothing. Not even a design. Nothing that looked like a button, or a lever, or a switch, or anything else that might help us to get out of there. The plan was a complete flop before it got started.

We gave up, finally, and scouted the rest of the roof. There, too, we drew a complete blank. There was nothing that could help us. The roof was a plain, featureless rectangle, with the box-like "elevator" cage in the center, grassy turf covering its whole surface and the sheer, frightening drop of a mile on all sides.

Cleelock lying on his belly while Duncan and I sat on his heels reported that he could see no windows over the edge. And, even if he had, we scarcely could have reached them. We had no ladder. The grass could not well have been plaited into a rope, though we thought of it—it was about the consistency of boiled asparagus. I suppose we could have tied our belts together—but what could we have moored them to?

No, there was no way of getting off that roof. And there was also nothing to eat.

We sat in front of the sealed door and waited for something to happen. Duncan said speculatively, "I bet they find us pretty quick. There were only about two hundred buttons in the car: Trial and error will do it."

Hopefully, I put in, "Well, maybe not. Most of the other floors—or whatever you call them—must offer a little more concealment than this one. They'll have to investigate every possibly hiding place, and that might take quite a while."

Duncan said tiredly, "All that means is that we have a chance of starving to death. The hell with it. We're not going anywhere—let's not kid ourselves."

We thought that over for a while in silence. I squinted up at the lavender sky and saw that the sun—small at this distance, but bright—was rapidly approaching the horizon. By the conditioning of long habit, I began to feel sleepy.

"We ought to post a guard and turn in," I suggested.

Cleelock nodded drowsily and Duncan, who was still wide-awake, said, "All right. I'll take the first turn. You can go to sleep any time you like. But..." His eyes went to the edge of the roof, not twenty feet away. "...try not to roll out of bed!"

DUNCAN WAS nudging me, and I woke up. It was night, but there were more stars out than I had ever seen. Duncan's face was clearly visible in their light.

I yawned. "Did anything exciting happen?"

He shook his head. "Not a blame thing. Oh, there's something funny way off on the horizon. But it's not very exciting. Just a lot of reddish light—looks like a big fire, maybe."

I stood up and looked where he was pointing. The sky was discolored with savage red, silhouetting the elevator cage. But it was a long way off indeed. "Too far away to bother us," I said. "Okay, you can go to sleep; I'm awake now."

He lay down and I began walking around, wishing I had a cigarette.

It was becoming very cold indeed on the roof, and I was grateful for my leather flight jacket. I looked around me with some interest. Even though we were in the "We who are about to die—" category, it was still a unique situation, and I was curious about our surroundings.

Overhead, I saw, were the familiar constellations. I picked out the Dipper and the wobbly W of Cassiopeia, unchanged by a mere hundred-million-mile shift in parallax. They did seem oddly bright, though nothing else about them was strange. I could see easily the components of the binary in the cup of the dipper, and Arcturus, to the south, was almost too brilliant to look at. The thin atmosphere, I thought.

In the monochromatic starlight the blue of the grass faded out, and the gaily-colored towers that were all around us had bleached to a uniform gray. There was not a light in them. No windows, of course; I remembered that there had been no windows. But still, I would have expected some kind of light in a city, even if it were only reflected up from the ground below.

Greatly daring, I crawled on my hands and knees to the edge of the roof and looked down.

I am a phlegmatic type, I think; surely not one of those who suffer from desires to fling themselves off high places. But, looking down into that yawning ebony chasm in that deserted city, I felt the lure of it calling to me. It was so utterly, entirely black. Even the outlines of the adjacent structures faded into an inky pool. So black that it seemed a sort of midnight well, and I had the feeling that I could leap off into that thick, clinging vacuum and swim about in it.

But, fortunately, I didn't try it; I scuttled backward from the edge of the roof and stood up.

Utter blackness. It seemed we were in a ghost city. Not a sound, not a glimmer of light.

I HAD A sudden idea, and peered out toward where I had seen the cube city. It was still there and, sure enough, as I had expected it shone! There was life in that city, beyond doubt. There were no yellowish dots of luminescence such as you see in an Earthly skyline, no windows or lighted advertising signs. But a bluish glow pervaded it, outlining its box-like buildings clearly enough even at fifteen miles distance.

I had kept my watch running. The time it indicated, set to a time zone on a planet hundreds of millions of miles a way, meant nothing at all, but at least it could be used to give me an idea of the passing hours. Two hours of solitary vigil, I decided, would be plenty. Then I would let Cleelock take over.

I leaned against the "elevator" box and allowed myself to drift off into reverie. It was a pleasant feeling...until I caught myself just as I was falling forward onto my face, and knew I had almost been asleep. I roused myself and began walking around again.

The reddish glow was still silhouetting the box, but far brighter than before. Intrigued, I walked around the box.

A glowing semicircle of light burst upon me. The size of a hundred moons, blotched and streaked with red and purplish light.

It was Jupiter!

I stared at it in reverent fascination. A fantastic sight, even by the fantastic standards of the fantastic place we were in. I saw the, cloudy areas of its supposed continents and seas far more clearly than I remembered seeing them in the imaginative drawings I had cherished in my youth. So near and so huge—I almost imagined that I could reach out and thrust my fist through it.

"Jupiter," I whispered; "that cinches it." And at once the strangeness of our predicament reached me as it never had before. We were on Ganymede, all right...and a long, long way from home.

I kept my eyes on the tremendous disk, in absorption. By the time the two hours were up the roof was illuminated almost as brightly as by day, with the vast

Jovian circle staring down at us over the top of the elevator, Cleelock was stirring restlessly in the light, and I had no compunctions about waking him.

He stared round-eyed at the planet overhead. "What the devil!" he gasped.

I told him what it was and he nodded, wide-awake. Our voices woke Duncan and the three of us talked excitedly about the magnificent sight, until Duncan's practical mind took us onto a more urgent subject.

"Damn, but I'm hungry," he said ruefully.

That put the quietus on any further talk about abstractions. We were all hungry, and there seemed to be nothing we could do about it. Cleelock ordered, "Forget it. Go back to sleep."

It seemed to be the best advice possible under the circumstances and Duncan and I tried to put it into effect. But we didn't succeed. Because just as we lay down and closed our eyes we heard a surprised yelp from Cleelock and the metallic sound of a door sliding open.

We leaped to our feet. The door to the "elevator" box had opened. And out of it stepped our gorgeous, feather-haired traveling companion and her two-legged pet!

"GRAB HER, Tommy!" I yelled, and Cleelock jumped to do it. The girl's hand went to her mouth in shock and bewilderment, but she put up no resistance at all. After the initial surprise she merely stared at him with resigned loathing. Looking somewhat foolish, he released her arms after a moment and just stood there in an attitude of threat.

Duncan and I closed in on her, me waving my silly little knife. "Perfect!" Cleelock exulted. "We couldn't ask for anything more! The very person we want, and she comes walking into our arms!"

"What'll we do with her?" I asked.

Cleelock hesitated. "Well—make her take us to the ship."

"And how are we going to get that across to her?"

"I'll try," Duncan volunteered. He fixed the girl with his third-degree stare. "Do you speak English?" he demanded.

She looked at him in wondering silence.

"I said, do you speak English?" he repeated. *"Parlez-vous Francais? Panymayoo Parusski? Parlate Italiano? Sprechen sie Deutsch? Se habla—I* mean, *habla Espanol?"*

She frowned uncertainly, then essayed a peal of music.

Cleelock said, "Look, linguist, quit wasting time. Suppose she did speak one of those languages. What good would it do us? *We* don't."

Duncan shrugged uncomfortably. "Let me try again," he begged. He snapped his fingers to focus her attention, then made an effort at sign language. He pointed to the elevator door, then down, then to us, then up into the sky with a broad, sweeping motion. The girl gaped at him in bewilderment.

"You're doing fine," Cleelock said in disgust. "How do you expect her to figure that one out? I *know* what you're driving at, and even so those handies of yours confuse me." He scratched his head thoughtfully. "This palaver isn't getting us anywhere at all," he said. "Let's try direct action."

"Sure," Duncan said. "How?"

"We'll drag her into the elevator. Maybe she'll get the idea. If she doesn't, all right—we'll just keep pushing buttons till we get to where we want to go. And let's step on it—before somebody else decides to use the car again."

"Okay," I said—it was as good an idea as any. "What about the dog?"

"We'll leave that here," said Cleelock, the masterful. "Let me show you how."

HE ATTRACTED the girl's attention and pointed to the collar around her neck, gesturing her to take it off. She gazed wide-eyed, uncomprehending. He touched the dog-like beast, pointed to its collar, ran his finger along the leash to her own, repeated the take-off gesture.

Then she got it. She stumbled back in sheer horror. I cannot think of any obscene or menacing gesture he could have made that would have sparked a more horrified response in an Earth girl. The redhead's eyes were wide with fright and revulsion.

"Oh, Lord," groaned Cleelock. "Now what's the matter?" Impulsively, he grabbed the leash and yanked at it.

That did it. She shrieked in terror—which, incidentally, tore my heart out with compassion—and her hands flew helplessly to her throat. There was a *click* and the collar came off in her hands. She set it gently down on the ground, touched the beast in farewell, and waited for the worst.

"You see," bragged Cleelock, grinning broadly. "Now we can get going! Come on, you..." He prodded the girl toward the cab. "Let's make haste while Jupiter shines!"

She went without resistance, and the three of us followed close behind. When we were inside she looked up and saw the beast had been deserted, gazing after us with dimmed, mindless eyes. As she watched it looked away and, like a grazing sheep, began drifting over toward the edge of the building. Then she went wild.

"Hold onto her, Nick!" Cleelock yelled. "Don't let her out."

I had her—but she was a terrific, squirming handful. "She's afraid her pet will fall off the roof," I panted.

"Never mind that," Cleelock ordered. "We can't worry about him. Hang on." He stared at the array of buttons, reached up and touched one.

Just as his finger came to rest on it the girl gave a squawk like a steam calliope and broke loose. She lunged out of the door.

"Hey!" I yelled, and jumped after her. I brought her down with a flying tackle, but she wriggled free like a greased dolphin and chased after the animal, now perilously close to the unfenced edge of the roof.

I saw that she caught it and led it to safety. But it didn't matter particularly to me at that time.

Because, glancing over my shoulder, I also saw that the door to the elevator-thing had closed once more. And my friends, no doubt, were back in the other city, feeling as foolish, and lost, and worried as I was myself.

CHAPTER FIVE

THE redhead came ambling back to me, smiling happily, the silver collar of the dog's leash pressed lovingly to her throat. She didn't appear to resent the rough handling I'd given her at all.

I got up and brushed at the bluish grass stains on my legs. Candidly, I was worried. It had been bad enough with Cleelock and Duncan to share my misery, but with them gone off to heaven-knows-where it was far worse. Still", this was a remarkably pretty girl, I told myself, and the situation did have some attractive angles. In the ruby light from Jupiter, overhead the flaming crimson of her hair washed out, and she might have been an exceptionally fine-haired Terrestrial blonde.

She grinned at me in a friendly fashion and sang a questioning phrase.

"It beats me, honey," I told her. "Try singing it as a polka."

She looked at me blankly. I pointed to the closed door. "Open," I ordered, without much hope.

Another peal of music.

"I said *open*," I repeated. I remembered the knife and held it before me, pointed at her as menacingly as I could manage. "Open that door!"

No music this time. Instead, she laughed at me with broad good humor. When she was quite through laughing she reached out and plucked the knife from my incredulous fingers. She stared at it for a second, then negligently tossed it up and away. It sailed through the air, and dropped out of sight into the chasm beyond the edge of the roof. She watched it gravely, then turned and gave me another homefolks smile.

"Well, I looked good on that one, I must say," I said bitterly. "All right, pal. Now what shall we do?"

She patted my shoulder comfortingly. Then she handed me the silver collar.

I stood, holding it in my hand. It tingled oddly, almost as though charged with a minute electric current. I started to hand it back to her, a little nervously, but she halted me. She gestured the act of holding the thing to my throat, as she herself had been doing before.

"Huh?" I said.

A peal of peremptory music. She frowned and repeated the gesture.

"Oh, lady," I said, "I haven't got time for games. I've got a lot of worrying to catch up on." I handed the collar back to her and walked over to the closed door of the *soi-disant* elevator. I was running my hands over it for the twentieth hopeless time when she tapped me on the shoulder.

I turned. She was holding the collar out to me again, a beseeching, lost look in her eyes.

I began to lose my patience. "Good Lord," I said in exasperation. "Leave me alone." I walked away to stare off into the red-lit night at the distant city of cubes.

The black chasm, now shot through with a dull, mean-looking red, was below me. I looked into it—from a safe distance—with a sort of grim enjoyment. At least, I thought, I could always jump...

A gentle peal of music from behind me. I leaped a foot-away from the edge of the building.

She was holding the collar out to me again. I thought of a line from my high school Shakespeare. Something about, "thrice offering a kingly crown, which he did thrice refuse."

"Honey, *don't* sneak up behind me like that," I said.

She smiled forgivingly. Then, still smiling, she walked toward me, her arms outstretched to me. It was a strange time for romance, I thought.

But she stepped up close to me, until her small, pointed chin was only an inch from my breastbone. Her arms went about my neck. It took me a split fraction of a second to make up my mind what she was after, and that was entirely too much time.

My subconscious woke up and began squawking, *Danger!* But it was too late. I felt something chill and metallic circle my neck. There was an instant of numbing electrical shock; I heard the click as she fastened the catch...

And the collar was locked about my neck.

SOMEONE WAS speaking to me, not in words.

It was not a voice, but I under, stood it. It was not my own thoughts, but it was in my brain.

It was a thought, an emotion, and a mood. It was three things—or more than three things—expressed at once, yet each standing alone. There was a command of non-fear; a broad soundless laughter; a memory of my amusing obstinacy.

In English, it might have been said like this: *Do not be afraid. Earthman. You struggled very hard, but*—laughter—*the struggle is over.*

I stared incredulously at the girl. She was watching me with amusement on her delicately shaped face, but surely it

54

was not her thoughts that were invading my mind. "Who—who are you?" I said aloud.

Again that echoing laughter. Then suddenly a picture was in my mind, so vivid that it blotted out what my eyes were seeing and replaced the view with a vision of...of the pallid, deformed, dog-like thing to which I was leashed, in all its idiot hideousness!

I said feebly, "No. Oh, no!"

That is what I am, said the soundless voice in my brain, with sadness and humorous resignation woven into the meaning of the thought. *That is what my people have been for a million years.*

What happened then is an inglorious episode in my career, and I had rather not dwell on it. I was panic-stricken. Things were just suddenly too much for me...and I rebelled.

I clawed at the collar around my neck, fumbling for a catch that I couldn't find. I'm not sure, but I think that I must have been screaming. My fright awoke a responsive alarm in the mind that was within my mind, and I sensed that, for an infinitesimal second, it drew away in doubt.

Then...it returned, warm, strong, reassuring. *Sleep, Earthman,* said the voice in my mind with gentle solicitude. *Sleep—*

I slept.

THERE WERE chaotic dreams of things beyond my understanding, and a feeling of receiving instruction from a master. Then I was awake.

It wasn't a real sleep, I suppose. I don't think it could have lasted more than a moment, because when I opened my eyes there was no waking up drowsiness, and I saw that the girl was standing just as she had stood before, watching me expectantly.

"Is it over?" she asked.

I nodded, and started to reply, "Yes." But I did a rapid double take, which left me goggling at her. Her voice had been the peal of music—yet I had understood what she said:

She saw my confusion and, understanding, laughed. "I see that it is over," she said in that strange music, answering her own question. "How do you feel? Can you understand me?"

I nodded speechlessly.

"Then tell me how you feel," she demanded. "If you can understand, you can talk."

Well, that made sense, of course. But nevertheless, it was absurd. I tried, unbelievingly, to speak. And, though I could not have said how it happened, a musical phrase came to my mind, and I uttered it, and knew that it meant: "I feel fine!"

But it was a lie. I was dizzy, and bewildered beyond endurance.

I sat limply on the sparse blue grass. The movement tugged the leash about my neck, and the dog-beast—the thing that just had been inside my mind—croaked protestingly, then slid to its knees with a jolt and stared brainlessly around.

The girl said, "Here—let me take the collar off. He has withdrawn rapport. It is so difficult, the first time. It tires him, and it is bad for you."

I let her lean, strong fingers touch something in the collar. It fell into jointed halves, and she held it in her hand. She was smiling at me.

"Tell me what this is all about," I begged her.

She hesitated, and then she began to tell me.

I was in a plastic, credulous mood, and if what she said had been obvious fabrication I would have believed it anyway, for lack of the will to doubt. But it was clearly, fantastically the truth.

"First," she said, "you are in no danger. There was some danger but it has passed. There was the danger that your mind would not survive the contact with the mind of the Khreen."

"Khreen?" It was a warbling, ascending musical note, the same word the Boss had used back in the rocket. I waved at the drowsing beast. "Do you mean *that?*"

"Yes," she said. She looked at the animal, and in her look I saw both tenderness and genuine respect. Respect for that hunk of low-grade beast!

"Explain this to me," I begged.

SHE TOUCHED the beast fondly. "A million years ago," she said, "Ganymede was a civilized world. Its people were humanoid—more like myself, I think, than like you. And they were advanced in science, as you can see." She hesitated, then went on, and by and by I began to understand. There was a reason why that hulk of an animal could command respect and affection from as brilliant a girl as she. For it was a beast, all right...but, it was also the finest mind the universe had ever spawned!

"Perhaps," she said, "their science was too far advanced. They knew ways of changing the stuff of life itself—radiations, surgical techniques, things I cannot understand. And through that came their great catastrophe."

The Khreen, as I learned to call them, had grown and matured, covering their own planet with their works and sending scouts to every planet of the system. But they had found—nothing. Half the worlds were bleak ice; some were roaring inferno. Two—Earth and Venus—showed life, but nothing that could be called intelligence.

Thwarted in the search for another race's companionship, they returned to their own world, determined to create an intelligent race! One by one they examined and tested the life forms of their planet, and one by one they were discarded. Until they came to a small-brained amphibian, rust-colored and few in numbers, that lived in their swamps. It was the thing they sought, far enough along the road of evolution to be of value, and yet it had not specialized.

They took that little rust-colored reptile from the swamps and put it in their laboratories. They charted a path for its evolution to follow, and started it on the way with their miraculous rays.

Then, something went wrong.

"It seemed to be a self-sustaining reaction," the girl said slowly. "I—I'm not sure exactly what happened, because the knowledge of it was lost in the upheaval that followed, and I probably could not understand anyhow. But the rays went wild. And all over Ganymede, evolution was uncontrolled."

I took in the meaning of her words slowly. It was a horrible vision that they conjured up. As she spoke, I imagined free mutation of species, monsters being born.

It had not lasted long, she told me, but in the brief time that the rays were loose in the world, it destroyed their status quo. In effect, a sentence of execution had been passed on every person and every beast that was alive on Ganymede, and it was only a matter of waiting until the corpses cooled. For slow, horrible radiation burns destroyed them.

Within a year the only living things were the newborn", and they were monstrous.

"Every species threw off mutants," she said. "Uncounted hundreds of thousands of them. Some had many heads, or no limbs at all; some had rubbery skeletons, some were born insane, lived insane, died insane. Some were sterile, and they died. Some were just never meant to live...and they died. Of all the thousands of new types that the rays spawned, only two found mates, and bred true, and survived. One was the Khreen—" she patted the dog-beast. "The other was what you call the pinkies—the descendants of the little red reptile that started the whole thing."

I shook my head wonderingly. Then, as I remembered something, I said, "The Boss was telling me something like this once. He started to tell about a race that was in solitary confinement for a million years. I didn't understand at the time, and I don't now. Is this what he was talking about?"

She nodded. "That was the horror of the whole thing," she said seriously. "For the Khreen came to look like animals, but they were not animals. They survived the rays—but their tragedy was almost worse than if they had become extinct."

I stared incredulously at the dog-beast. "You say this isn't an animal? Well, it would have fooled me. Did—did the rays work in reverse, maybe—making it an atavism or something?"

"No," she said. "The rays did their work, only too well. The Khreen evolved far beyond humanity. What you see before you is superman."

I laughed tentatively. "Sure," I said, going along with the gag. "I can tell that just by looking."

"Really," she said, and I saw that she was not joking. "The Khreen evolved, but in an unfortunate direction. The brain of the Khreen became a marvelous instrument for pure thought. The body—evolved too. You know that, even in your own body and mine, some of the work of directing your actions is done by what you call reflexes?"

"Yes."

"And that these reflexes are not in the brain, but in a group of nerves in your spinal column?"

"I'd heard that," I admitted.

She nodded decisively. "Well, in the evolved body of the Khreen, the work of that group of motor-nerves was increased sharply. In fact—it took over every physical function. The nerves that led to the brain itself atrophied and disappeared. The body became independent, with its own tiny 'brain', a separate nerve system, complete control of its musculature. The brain and the body became separate individuals...and the result was a godlike mind, in the body of a beast!"

"Good Lord," I said.

I LAY BACK, staring up at the round face of Jupiter overhead, thinking it over. Questions flooded into my brain—too many for me to ask even one, because each question was driven out by a dozen new ones before I could get it to my lips. I felt benumbed and bewildered...and a physical thing, forcing itself to my consciousness, was demanding more and more attention. I was hungry.

I stood up, and I felt faint. Small wonder—since the pinkies had awakened us in the space ship, I had had but two meals!

The girl saw me reeling. "What is the matter?" she asked in musical alarm.

"Nothing much," I said apologetically. "I'm just hungry."

"Hungry? Oh." She frowned at me in concentration. "We—we don't eat, here," she said finally. "Still, I suppose—"

"Don't eat?" I yelped. "How do you survive?"

"Why, we use the life-waters," she said, surprised. "Your food does nothing but supply you with energy and materials to replace wastage. The life-waters do the same thing. Only much more simply—by absorption through the skin—and without the contamination in ordinary food. Also, they have a germicidal effect," she added delicately. "I understand your system is flooded with germs."

"Life-waters," I said, rolling the sound of it on my tongue. "Well, all right. Where do we go to find these life-waters?"

"On the roof of the Entrance Building, for one place," She gestured back to the cubical city. "Where you and your friends got so—ah—excited."

"Let's go," I said. "I'm game."

SHE WAVED her hand before the blank face of the "elevator" door—only she told me, when I asked her, that it was not an elevator but a matter transmitter. The door opened. No buttons, no nothing…it was some sort of electronic capacitance control, I suppose. Inside, with me and the Khreen crowding after her, she pressed a button and the door closed, opened, and we were back on the other roof again.

"Very clever piece of equipment," I said, staggering slightly in dizziness. Then, remembering, "By the way, you haven't told me how I learned to speak your language."

"The Khreen taught you, of course. Telepathically, while you were wearing the collar. That's all the collar is—a telepathy-wave amplifier, and the wire is a conducting cable."

I started to ask more questions, but, "Later," she said firmly. "First get in the pool."

I looked around with a slight, involuntary shiver. There was no one else on the roof, just the two of us—and the Khreen. The pool, there before me, was just as I remembered it...limpid orange flame.

"Go ahead," she said. "It won't hurt you."

I hesitated. "All right. Shall I dive in with my clothes on?"

"Of course not! Take them off."

"Then turn your back," I said. "On that I insist."

The shrug of her shoulders denoted complete lack of comprehension, but, after giving me a wondering gaze, she complied. "How long must I stand like this?" she asked plaintively.

"I'll tell you when to turn around," I said...

It took me several seconds to get up my nerve, but finally I jumped.

The liquid was warm—that was my first impression. Other than that, it felt like nothing at all, except plain water. I was a little disappointed.

It was curiously soothing, though. I lay back in it, relaxed and floating, and new strength seeped back into me. I felt warm, sheltered, comfortable. Almost I could have drifted off to sleep...

"Can I turn around yet?" the girl demanded.

I blinked and splashed myself to a standing position. "Nope! But tell me, how long to stay in this?"

She said, "As long as you like. You've been in it long enough for about three days, though—you might as well come out."

Obediently I crawled out, scraped the golden, fiery drops off me with the flat of my hand, climbed back into my clothing. I felt like a new man.

I looked at her with revived appreciation. "Say," I asked, "have you got a name?"

"A name?" Puzzlement in the musical voice. "No."

"Then I'll give you one," I decided. "I think I'll call you—Honey."

She repeated the English word. Her attempts were amusing, but I had another question on my mind and couldn't take time to laugh at her.

"You forgot to tell me your own story," I reminded her. "What about it?"

SHE TURNED around and looked at me. She said, "I don't know my story. Only what the pinkies have told me. You see, I was very young when I came here."

"From Earth?"

She nodded. "The first expedition. The one that brought you back was the second. They found me and my parents, and took us here—for curiosities mostly, I think, but also to use in their laboratories."

I grimaced. "That doesn't sound very good," I observed. "You mean, to cut up?"

"Oh, no. The Khreen are still trying to control the evolutionary rays. They could do nothing with my parents, because they were mature, fully formed. On myself, they say, they had limited success." She touched her corona of pinkish, feather-light hair. "You are too old too," she added, smiling elfin; "they were so disappointed!"

"Yeah, but what about your parents? What happened to them?"

"They died," she said sadly. "When I was very young. Oh, it was not the fault of the Khreen. They were sick when they were found, and they could not be saved."

I nodded. It checked well enough, and I was relieved to find that, after all, she at least had once been human. I *wanted* her to be human...

But I had one more question. "You said the Khreen were in solitary confinement, didn't you? What did you mean?"

She said, "Oh, that is over now. But for almost a million years, they neither saw, nor heard, nor felt anything. They were telepathic among themselves, and they could communicate mind to mind. But you see, on the whole planet there was no other mind at all that they could reach?"

"Not even the pinkies?"

"Not at first. After a long, long time the pinkies began to have intelligence. The rays gave them a good start, but it was not quite enough. It took almost a million years until their brains were fully enough developed to receive the thoughts of the Khreen. Even today, it is not perfect. That is why they—and we—use these." She touched the silver collar of the beast, which was apparently asleep on the ground beside us.

"But once the pinkies had attained intelligence," she went on, "it was simple. Contact was still very incomplete, but some of the pinkies turned out to be sensitives, and the Khreen began to suggest things to their minds. The first step..." She smiled at the thought. "...was to persuade them to domesticate the Khreen!"

"You mean, use them for, something?"

"Yes. As beasts of burden. It didn't harm the minds of the Khreen, of course—they could feel nothing. And it kept the two races together, until the Khreen had time to teach them something of science, and develop the thought-collar for better control. They were helped a lot by the fact that their cities still stood, and some of their tools were still in them."

I looked around me. "Is this one of them?"

Her face registered faint revulsion. "No. This is what the pinkies built for themselves. So ugly! But the other city—where we were just now—that is one of the old ones. Much more beautiful. I go there often."

She stopped talking, and I began to pace around, digesting her information. It was hard to believe, but it had to be true. Everything fitted. Nothing that would fit the facts could be any less fantastic.

I spotted Cleelock's discarded knife where he had thrown it, and idly picked it up. Then I had an idea.

"Say," I said, "why couldn't the Khreen use this telepathy gadget on their own brains? Not the real brains—the others, the ones that control the bodies?"

She shook her head. "Telepathy," she reminded me, "can only occur between two full-fledged mature minds. The body brains are very rudimentary, really. They hope, perhaps some day, to evolve a little farther...but they were afraid to take the chance on another catastrophe like the one before. However, they do perform experiments—such as the one on me."

I was about to speak, but something halted me. Something that was prodding at my brain—as though someone were shouting at me, urgently, soundlessly, a long way off.

I turned to the girl, and she had felt it too. Her eyes went wide with self-reproach.

"The Khreen!" she gasped suddenly. "I've been out of rapport—"

She clutched at the collar of the neglected genius-beast—still asleep, to all external appearances—beside her. She snapped it around her neck, close to the medulla oblongata. I realized, and began "talking" to the alert mind within the sleeping beast. I saw an expression of surprise and alarm cross her face, and she stared at me almost with hostility.

"What's the matter?" I asked anxiously.

She frowned in agitation. "Your friends are in trouble!" she said. "They've managed, somehow, to get into the rocket ship. They've closed the ports—and they're trying to take off!"

"The fools!" I groaned. "They can't possibly fly it; they'll be killed!"

"Of course," she said soberly. "But that's not the worst. One of the Khreen is trapped inside!"

CHAPTER SIX

We were back in the "elevator" in a fraction of a moment, all three of us. Before I had a chance to collect my thoughts the door was open again, and we were back in the corridor on the ground floor.

As before, the canoe-shaped car was waiting for us, with a pinky in it at the controls. He was working up a fit of fury, and when he saw me it exploded. "Savages! Cannibals! Murderers!" he yelled, and by the tone, even more than by the fact that he spoke in English, I knew him as the Boss.

"Quiet down," I advised him, speaking in the musical tongue so that the girl could understand. "I didn't do anything."

"Hah!" he said bitterly. "You are all alike, you specimens. Fiends!"

"Leave us not call names, Boss." I begged. "All they're trying to do is get away from here; you can't blame them for that."

"Yes I can!"

"Well, it's your own fault," I said wearily. "You scared us half to death, you and your bad manners. What happened?"

"Bad things happened! The two fiends came out of that building over there—" he pointed with his webbed paw. "One of us saw them, but by the time he was able to get a car to chase them, they were halfway to the ship, jumping along like anything. Great big fiends!"

"Well, let's get out there," I said.

"Maybe I can talk sense into their heads. Though, heaven knows, you've made it a tough job."

He snarled at me. "Get in," he said sourly.

We did, and he played with the board in front of him. The car zoomed ahead, swerved in a racing turn and scooted for the purple rocket.

"What's the score?" I yelled to the girl over the noise of the wind rushing past. "Can they see us coming?"

She shook her head. "There's no way of contacting them from outside."

"Great!" I said in surprise and chagrin. "Then what's the sense of coming out here?"

She explained hastily, "I mean, as long as we're on the ground. There is one way you can attract their attention. You'll have to climb up the nose of the ship to where the piloting compartment is—the Khreen who's trapped inside thinks that that's where they are, according to the telepathic messages he sent to my Khreen. Once you're up there, they'll be able to see you through the nose of the ship. There's a port that will open when they release it from inside—" She described the port to me.

I said, "Well, it sound, easy enough. What's the catch?"

She looked at me with sorrow and a trace of fear—not fear for herself, I thought exultantly, but for *me*. "The catch is that they are trying to get the ship started. And if they do—"

She bit her lip and didn't finish the sentence.

She didn't have to. I swallowed with some difficulty. "I see what you mean," I said. "If they win, I lose."

THE BOSS brought the car to a stop that would have taken a quarter of an inch of rubber off the tires, if it had

had rubber tires. We were under the looming nose of the ship.

The girl pointed, and I recognized the bulging glassy panel behind which lay the pilot chamber. There were metal hoops and projections spotted all over the hull, apparently to help maintenance crews. It wouldn't be very difficult to climb, in this light gravity.

I grabbed the first hoop and started lifting myself.

The girl spoke from behind me, her voice gentle. "Nick—" she pronounced it *Neek*. "Wait a moment, Neek."

I turned and let myself down again. She was out of the car, standing close with an expectant look on her face, arms half stretched out to me. She appeared exactly like a girl who wanted to be kissed. I kissed her. The appearance was not deceiving.

"Neek," she whispered, "please don't get hurt. Please."

I said, with a sort of speech impediment that I'd just picked up, "I'll try. Hey—where are you going?" She had released me, was getting back in the car.

"I must get out of blast range," she said sorrowfully, pointing at the beast in the car. "I can't endanger the Khreen. But please be safe, Neek."

I didn't waste time looking after her, but I kept an ear cocked to the dwindling sounds of the car as I began the twenty-foot climb.

It couldn't have taken more than a minute, but it was one of the very longest minutes of my life. I was expecting the worst. Vivid pictures flashed through my mind of what I would look like if Cleelock and Duncan got the rockets working before I could stop them. There were several possibilities, and I didn't like any of them. The blast of the rockets might get me, in which case I'd be a charred cinder;

or if I managed to hold on until the ship attained some altitude and then fell, I'd be a battered pulp. The very best I could hope for, I decided, would be to hang on until they reached outer space...in which case I would become a bloated icicle.

But by the time I had reviewed the chances, I had made it. I was clinging to the edge of the transparent cone at the nose of the ship.

Through the crystal I could see Duncan and Cleelock, furiously, working over the gadgets on the ship's control panel. By the express ions of exasperation and anxiety on their faces, they were exhorting each other to greater speed.

I banged on the window with all my strength. Nothing happened. I might as well have been sledging a bank vault with a marshmallow hammer, for all the noise I made. I yelled, but that was hopeless—they obviously couldn't hear me, because I couldn't hear them. Then I had a brilliant stroke of memory.

Cleelock's knife, which I had picked up on the roof, was still in my pocket. I took it out and hefted it. It was small, but it was made of a heavy metal, and would do the trick. I swung it against the glass.

It wasn't glass, or it would have broken. It didn't break; it gave out a low, bell-like tone, and wasn't even scratched. But inside, they heard it.

They gaped at me as if I'd been an orange-eyed monster with black wings. But finally I got it through their thick skulls that I wanted in, and how they were to accomplish same.

I tumbled inside, breathing hard in relief. "Where'd you come from?" Duncan demanded suspiciously.

"Climbed up the outside," I explained. "Listen, I've been talking to the Khreen—"

Cleelock cut in, "Never mind that! Do you know how to run one of these things?"

"No, of course not," I said. "But it doesn't matter. I tell you, I've been talking to the Khreen; you haven't got a thing to worry about. They look like beasts, I admit, but actually they're intelligent, and cultured, and—"

Cleelock's jaw was hanging as he stared at me in mixed incredulity and alarm. "Have you gone off your rocker?" he demanded. "Are you talking about those Ganymedan hairlesses?"

"Sure. I know they don't look like much, but they mean well. They've got two brains, see? And the good brain is terrific, only it doesn't have anything to do with the body."

Duncan said positively, "He's cracked under the strain. Should we tie him up, or something?"

Cleelock shook his head, keeping his eyes on me warily. "He's just excited," he said charitably. "Come on, let's get on with this thing; I want to go home."

They pushed me aside and returned to the instrument board. "Try those," Cleelock suggested, pointing to a bank of red studs on the right. Duncan began jabbing them at random, in a close approach to panic.

"Hold on, fellow," I said. They snarled over their shoulders at me.

"Well," I said, "if you want to be unreasonable." I hefted the butt of the knife in my hand. With my fist closed over it, its mass converted my hand into an effective blackjack.

I selected the proper, non-lethal spot at the back of their skulls. "This hurts me more than it does you," I murmured to their backs, raising my hand for the knockout tap...

*　　*　　*

WELL, THAT was all some time ago. We've been on Ganymede pretty near a year now, and heaven only knows how long the trip out from Earth took—about a year, anyway. The Boss told me once, but he expressed it as a fraction of Jupiter's year, and we all scratched our heads for about an hour trying to remember how long Jupiter's year was. Then we gave up.

We were all lolling around the life-water pool, one morning after *carna* but just before the time to *brust,* and Duncan said, "No matter how you figure it, we've been away close on to two years. I'm beginning to feel a little homesick."

We nodded. "I wonder how the Dodgers are making out," Tommy said. "And the cold war—how do you suppose that's doing?"

"Yeah," Duncan said wistfully, kicking his Feet into the pool and spraying orange sparks about. "It would be nice to go back."

I said, "It sure would. For one thing, I'd like to do something about—well, about legalizing—that is, I mean—" I trailed off, pointing to Honey, who was staring dreamily at the lavender sky. Cleelock and Duncan nodded, understanding perfectly. Cleelock said:

"I had a girl myself back in Memphis. Hope she's still there." He looked wistful for a moment. "In fact," he said, "I hope *Memphis* is still there."

Honey took her eyes off the sky and tossed back her gorgeous hair. In singsong she said, "The Boss is going back to Earth on another sampling expedition soon. If you ask him, he'll probably bring a couple of extra girls for you."

72

"Ah!" said Tommy. Then, in English, "Maybe he could do better than that. Maybe he could bring us back to Earth."

Duncan nodded. "Back to Earth. That's where we belong, men. Back to San Diego, and that lovely fog that hangs over it all winter long. Back to Klotchweiler's store, and my old job behind the counter."

"Back," I said, "to work. To getting up when the alarm goes off and fighting my way onto the Sea Beach Express. Back to sinus trouble and the atomic bomb. And hash house food. And insomnia and water shortages."

"And coal strikes and steel strikes," Tommy supplied, "and phone strikes and train strikes and—"

"And income tax," said Duncan. "Don't forget the income tax. Don't ever forget the income tax."

Tommy stood up and shook his head like a man coming out of a dream. "Leave this planet and go back to Earth," he breathed, and looked at us wide-eyed. "Fellows, who are we *kidding?*"

THE END

If you've enjoyed this book, you will not want to miss these terrific titles…

ARMCHAIR SCI-FI & HORROR DOUBLE NOVELS, $12.95 each

D-1 **THE GALAXY RAIDERS** by William P. McGivern
SPACE STATION #1 by Frank Belknap Long

D-2 **THE PROGRAMMED PEOPLE** by Jack Sharkey
SLAVES OF THE CRYSTAL BRAIN by Rog Phillips

D-3 **YOU'RE ALL ALONE** by Fritz Leiber
THE LIQUID MAN by Bernard C. Gilford

D-4 **CITADEL OF THE STAR LORDS** by Edmond Hamilton
VOYAGE TO ETERNITY by Milton Lesser

D-5 **IRON MEN OF VENUS** by Don Wilcox
THE MAN WITH ABSOLUTE MOTION by Noel Loomis

D-6 **WHO SOWS THE WIND...** by Rog Phillips
THE PUZZLE PLANET by Robert A. W. Lowndes

D-7 **PLANET OF DREAD** by Murray Leinster
TWICE UPON A TIME by Charles L. Fontenay

D-8 **THE TERROR OUT OF SPACE** by Dwight V. Swain
QUEST OF THE GOLDEN APE by Paul W. Fairman & Milton Lesser

D-9 **SECRET OF MARRACOTT DEEP** by Henry Slesar
PAWN OF THE BLACK FLEET by Mark Clifton.

D-10 **BEYOND THE RINGS OF SATURN** by Robert Moore Williams
A MAN OBSESSED by Alan E. Nourse

ARMCHAIR SCIENCE FICTION CLASSICS, $12.95 each

C-1 **THE GREEN MAN**
by Harold M. Sherman

C-2 **A TRACE OF MEMORY**
By Keith Laumer

C-3 **INTO PLUTONIAN DEPTHS**
by Stanton A. Coblentz

ARMCHAIR MASTERS OF SCIENCE FICTION SERIES, $16.95 each

M-1 **MASTERS OF SCIENCE FICTION, Vol. One**
Bryce Walton—"Dark of the Moon" and other tales

M-2 **MASTERS OF SCIENCE FICTION, Vol. Two**
Jerome Bixby—"One Way Street" and other tales

If you've enjoyed this book, you will not want to miss these terrific titles...

ARMCHAIR SCI-FI & HORROR DOUBLE NOVELS, $12.95 each

D-91   **THE TIME TRAP** by Henry Kuttner
          THE LUNAR LICHEN by Hal Clement

D-92   **SARGASSO OF LOST STARSHIPS** by Poul Anderson
          THE ICE QUEEN by Don Wilcox

D-93   **THE PRINCE OF SPACE** by Jack Williamson
          POWER by Harl Vincent

D-94   **PLANET OF NO RETURN** by Howard Browne
          THE ANNIHILATOR COMES by Ed Earl Repp

D-95   **THE SINISTER INVASION** by Edmond Hamilton
          OPERATION TERROR by Murray Leinster

D-96   **TRANSIENT** by Ward Moore
          THE WORLD-MOVER by George O. Smith

D-97   **FORTY DAYS HAS SEPTEMBER** by Milton Lesser
          THE DEVIL'S PLANET by David Wright O'Brien

D-98   **THE CYBERENE** by Rog Phillips
          BADGE OF INFAMY by Lester del Rey

D-99   **THE JUSTICE OF MARTIN BRAND** by Raymond A. Palmer
          BRING BACK MY BRAIN by Dwight V. Swain

D-100   **WIDE-OPEN PLANET** by L. Sprague de Camp
          AND THEN THE TOWN TOOK OFF by Richard Wilson

ARMCHAIR SCIENCE FICTION CLASSICS, $12.95 each

C-31   **THE GOLDEN GUARDSMEN**
          by S. J. Byrne

C-32   **ONE AGAINST THE MOON**
          by Donald A. Wollheim

C-33   **HIDDEN CITY**
          by Chester S. Geier

ARMCHAIR SCI-FI & HORROR GEMS SERIES, $12.95 each

G-9   **SCIENCE FICTION GEMS, Vol. Five**
          Clifford D. Simak and others

G-10   **HORROR GEMS, Vol. Five**
          E. Hoffman Price and others

If you've enjoyed this book, you will not want to miss these terrific titles...

ARMCHAIR SCI-FI & HORROR DOUBLE NOVELS, $12.95 each

D-111 **THE MOON ERA** by Jack Williamson
REVENGE OF THE ROBOTS by Howard Browne

D-112 **SON OF THE BLACK CHALICE** by Milton Lesser
SENTRY OF THE SKY by Evelyn E. Smith

D-113 **OUTPOST ON THE MOON** by Joslyn Maxwell
POTENTIAL ZERO by S. J. Byrne

D-114 **OUTPOST INFINITY** by Raymond F. Jones
THE WHITE INVADERS by Ray Cummings

D-115 **TIME TRAP** by Rog Phillips
THE COSMIC DESTROYER by Alexander Blade

D-116 **THE OTHER SIDE OF THE MOON** by Edmond Hamilton
SECRET INVASION by Walter Kubilius

D-117 **DANGER MOON** by Frederik Pohl
THE HIDDEN UNIVERSE by Ralph Milne Farley

D-118 **THE WAILING ASTEROID** by Murray Leinster
THE WORLD THAT COULDN'T BE by Clifford D. Simak

D-119 **THE WHISPERING GORILLA** by Don Wilcox
RETURN OF THE WHISPERING GORILLA by David V. Reed

D-120 **SPECIAL EFFECT** by J. F. Bone
WARLORD OF KOR by Terry Carr

ARMCHAIR SCIENCE FICTION CLASSICS, $12.95 each

C-37 **THE GREEN MAN RETURNS**
by Harold M. Sherman

C-38 **THE SHAVER MYSTERY, Book Five**
by Richard S, Shaver

C-39 **MARS CHILD**
by Cyril Judd

ARMCHAIR MASTERS OF SCIENCE FICTION SERIES, $16.95 each

MS-9 **MASTERS OF SCIENCE FICTION AND FANTASY, Vol. Nine**
Poul Anderson, "The Star Beast" and other tales

MS-10 **MASTERS OF SCIENCE FICTION, Vol. Ten**
Robert Moore Williams, "Time Tolls for Toro" and other tales

If you've enjoyed this book, you will not want to miss these terrific titles...

ARMCHAIR SCI-FI & HORROR DOUBLE NOVELS, $12.95 each

FEAR RIDES THE ROCKETS...

That bastion of interplanetary space medics, the Interstellar Medical Service, was about the only remaining galactic organization that the hundreds of inhabited planets still respected. So when their service broke down in faraway Star Sector Twelve, it soon created the most dangerous of situations. When Calhoun took his Med ship out of overdrive near that sector's planet, Weald, he was only vaguely aware of the risks. But the crisis came home to him with a thundering crash the moment he radioed in for landing coordinates...

"Contamination! Full mobilization! Red alert! Death to blueskins!" Such were the nature of his greetings. And it began to look like a case of the cosmic jitters that only the most drastic of orbital surgery could cure.

ABOUT MURRAY LEINSTER

Murray Leinster...

...was born William F. Jenkins on June 16th, 1896 in Norfolk, Va. His writing career began in 1916 with the publishing of his first story, "The Foreigner" in *The Smart Set* magazine. Although he is considered one of the great writers of the science fiction genre, in his early years Leinster wrote many tales in other genres: jungle, mystery, horror, and western. Leinster broke into the science fiction field with his story, "The Runaway Skyscraper," which appeared in a 1919 issue of *Argosy* magazine. During the '30s, '40s, '50s, and '60s Leinster was a regular contributor to well-known pulp and digest magazines such as *Astounding Stories, Amazing Stories,* and *Weird Tales.* Leinster is considered the father of "parallel universe" stories with the publication of his 1934 story, "Sidewise in Time." During his long career Leinster was nominated for many writing awards, including the coveted Hugo Award, which he won in 1956 for his novelette, "Exploration Team." During his science fiction career, Leinster published over 30 novels and over 170 short stories. He passed away on June 8th, 1975.

THIS WORLD
IS TABOO

By
MURRAY LEINSTER

ARMCHAIR FICTION
PO Box 4369, Medford, Oregon 97504

For more information about Armchair Books and products, visit our website at…

www.armchairfiction.com

Or email us at…

armchairfiction@yahoo.com

CHAPTER ONE

The little Med Ship came out of overdrive and the stars were strange and the Milky Way seemed unfamiliar. Which, of course, was because the Milky Way and the local Cepheid marker-stars were seen from an unaccustomed angle and a not-yet-commonplace pattern of varying magnitudes.

But Calhoun grunted in satisfaction. There was a banded sun off to port, which was good. A breakout at no more than sixty light-hours from one's destination wasn't bad, in a strange sector of the galaxy and after three light-years of journeying blind.

"Arise and shine, Murgatroyd," said Calhoun. "Comb your whiskers. Get set to astonish the natives!"

A sleepy, small, shrill voice said: *"Chee!"*

Murgatroyd the *tormal* came crawling out of the small cubbyhole which was his own. He blinked at Calhoun.

"We're due to land shortly," Calhoun observed. "You will impress the local inhabitants. I will get unpopular. According to the records, there's been no Med Ship inspection here for twelve standard years. And that was practically no inspection, to judge by the report."

Murgatroyd said: *"Chee-chee!"*

He began to make his toilet, first licking his right-hand whiskers and then his left. Then he stood up and shook himself and looked interestedly at Calhoun. *Tormals* are companionable small animals. They are charmed when somebody speaks to them. They find great, deep satisfaction in imitating the actions of humans, as parrots and mynahs and parakeets imitate human speech. But *tormals* have certain valuable, genetically transmitted talents which make them much more valuable than mere companions or pets.

Calhoun got a light-reading for the banded sun. It could hardly be an accurate measure of distance, but it was a guide.

"Hold on to something, Murgatroyd!" he said.

Murgatroyd watched. He saw Calhoun make certain gestures which presaged discomfort. He popped back into his cubbyhole. Calhoun threw the overdrive switch and the Med Ship flicked back into that questionable state of being in which velocities of hundreds of times that of light are possible. The sensation of going into overdrive was unpleasant. A moment later, the sensation of coming out was no less so. Calhoun had experienced it often enough, and still didn't like it.

The sun Weald burned huge and terrible in space. It was close, now. Its disk covered half a degree of arc.

"Very neat," observed Calhoun. "Weald Three is our port, Murgatroyd. The plane of the ecliptic would be... Hmmm..."

He swung the outside electron telescope, picked up a nearby bright object, enlarged its image to show details, and checked it against the local star-pilot. He calculated a moment. The distance was too short for even the briefest of overdrive hops, but it would take time to get there on solar-system drive.

He thumbed down the communicator button and spoke into a microphone.

"Med Ship *Aesclipus Twenty* reporting arrival and asking coordinates for landing," he said matter-of-factly. "Purpose of landing is planetary health inspection. Our mass is fifty tons, standard. We should arrive at a landing position in something under four hours. Repeat. Med Ship *Aesclipus Twenty...*"

He finished the regular second transmission and made coffee for himself while he waited for an answer. Murgatroyd came out for a cup of coffee for himself. Murgatroyd adored coffee. In minutes he held a tiny cup in a furry small paw and sipped gingerly at the hot liquid.

A voice came out of the communicator:

"*Aesclipus Twenty*, repeat your identification."

Calhoun went to the control board.

"*Aesclipus Twenty*," he said patiently, "is a Med Ship, sent by the Interstellar Medical Service to make a planetary health inspection on Weald. Check with your public health authorities. This is the first Med Ship visit in twelve standard years, I believe—which is inexcusable. But your health authorities will know all about it. Check with them."

The voice said truculently:

"What was your last port?"

Calhoun named it. This was not his home sector, but Sector Twelve had gotten into a very bad situation. Some of its planets had gone unvisited for as long as twenty years, and twelve between inspections was almost commonplace. Other sectors had been called on to help it catch up.

Calhoun was one of the loaned Med Ship men, and because of the emergency he'd been given a list of half a dozen planets to be inspected one after another, instead of reporting back to sector headquarters after each visit. He'd had minor troubles before with landing-grid operators in Sector Twelve.

So he was very patient. He named the planet last inspected, the one from which he'd set out for Weald Three. The voice from the communicator said sharply:

"What port before that?"

Calhoun named the one before the last.

"Don't drive any closer," said the voice harshly, "or you'll be destroyed!"

Calhoun said coldly, "Listen, my fine feathered friend! I'm from the Interstellar Medical Service. You get in touch with planetary health services immediately! Remind them of the Interstellar Medical Inspection Agreement, signed on Tralee two hundred and forty standard years ago. Remind them that if they do not cooperate in medical inspection that I can put your planet under quarantine and your space commerce will be cut off like that!

"No ship will be cleared for Weald from any other planet in the galaxy until there has been a health inspection! Things have pretty well gone to pot so far as the Med Service in this sector is concerned, but it's being straightened up. I'm helping straighten it! I give you twenty minutes to clear this! Then I am coming in, and if I'm not landed a quarantine goes on! Tell your health authorities that!"

Silence. Calhoun clicked off and poured himself another cup of coffee. Murgatroyd held out his cup for a refill. Calhoun gave it to him.

"I hate to put on an official hat, Murgatroyd," he said, annoyed, "but there are some people who demand it. The rule is, never get official if you can help it, but when you must, out-official the official who's officialing you."

Murgatroyd said *"Chee!"* and sipped at his cup.

Calhoun checked the course of the Med Ship. It bore on through space. There were tiny noises from the communicator. There were whisperings and rustlings and the occasional strange and sometimes beautiful musical notes whose origin is yet obscure, but which, since they are carried by electromagnetic radiation of wildly varying wave lengths, are not likely to be the fabled music of the spheres.

In fifteen minutes a different voice came from the speaker.

"Med Ship *Aesclipus*! Med Ship *Aesclipus*!"

Calhoun answered and the voice said anxiously:

"Sorry about the challenge, but we have the blueskin problem always with us. We have to be extremely careful! Will you come in, please?"

"I'm on my way," said Calhoun.

"The planetary health authorities," said the voice, more anxiously still, "are very anxious to be cooperative. We need Med Service help! We lose a lot of sleep over the blueskin! Could you tell us the name of the last Med Ship to land here, and its inspector, and when that inspection was made? We want to look up the record of the event to be able to assist you in every possible way."

"He's lying," Calhoun told Murgatroyd, "but he's more scared than hostile."

He picked up the order folio on Weald Three. He gave the information about the last Med Ship visit.

"What?" he asked, "is a blueskin?"

He'd read the folio on Weald, of course, but as the ship swam onward through emptiness he went through it again. The last medical inspection had been only perfunctory. Twelve years earlier—instead of three—a Med Ship had landed on Weald. There had been official conferences with health officials. There was a report on the birth rate, the death rate, the anomaly rate, and a breakdown of all reported communicable diseases. But that was all. There were no special comments and no overall picture.

Presently Calhoun found the word in a Sector dictionary, where words of only local usage were to be found:

"Blueskin: Colloquial term for a person recovered from a plague which left large patches of blue pigment irregularly distributed over the body. Especially, inhabitants of Dara. The condition is said to be caused by a chronic, nonfatal form of Dara plague and has been said to be noninfectious, though this is not certain. The etiology of Dara plague has not been worked out. The blueskin condition is hereditary but not a genetic modification, as markings appear in non-Mendelian distributions."

Calhoun puzzled over it. Nobody could have read the entire Sector directory, even with unlimited leisure during travel between solar systems. Calhoun hadn't tried. But now he went laboriously through indices and cross-references while the ship continued to travel onward.

He found no other reference to blueskins. He looked up Dara. It was listed as an inhabited planet, some four hundred years colonized, with a landing-grid and, at the time the main notice was written out, a flourishing interstellar commerce. But there was a memo, evidently added to the entry in some change of editions: *"Since plague, special license from Med Service is required for landing."*

That was all. Absolutely all.

The communicator said suavely:

"Med Ship *Aesclipus Twenty*! Come in on vision, please!"

Calhoun went to the control board and threw on vision.

"Well, what now?" he demanded.

His screen lighted. A bland face looked out at him.

"We have—ah—verified your statements," said the third voice from Weald. "Just one more item. Are you alone in your ship?"

"Of course," said Calhoun, frowning.

"Quite alone?" insisted the voice.

"Obviously!" said Calhoun.

"No other living creature?" insisted the voice again. "Of—oh!" said Calhoun, annoyed. He called over his shoulder. "Murgatroyd! Come here!"

Murgatroyd hopped to his lap and gazed interestedly at the screen. The bland face changed remarkably. The voice changed even more.

"Very good!" it said. "Very, very good! Blueskins do not have *tormals*! You are Med Service! By all means come in! Your coordinates will be…"

Calhoun wrote them down. He clicked off the communicator again and growled to Murgatroyd, "So I might have been a blueskin, eh? And you're my passport, because only Med Ships have members of your tribe aboard! What the hell's the matter, Murgatroyd? They act like they think somebody's trying to get down on their planet with a load of plague germs!"

He grumbled to himself for minutes. The life of a Med Ship man is not exactly a sinecure, at best. It means long periods in empty space in overdrive, which is absolute and deadly tedium. Then two or three days aground, checking official documents and statistics, and asking questions to see how many of the newest medical techniques have reached this planet or that, and the supplying of information about such as have not arrived.

Then the lifting out to space for long periods of tedium, to repeat the process somewhere else. Med Ships carry only one man because two could not stand the close contact without quarreling with each other. But Med Ships do carry *tormals*, like Murgatroyd, and a *tormal* and a man can get along indefinitely, like a man and a dog. It is a highly unequal friendship, but it seems to be satisfactory to both.

Calhoun was very much annoyed with the way the Med Service had been operated in Sector Twelve. He was one of many men at work to correct the results of incompetence in directing Med Service in this sector. But it is always disheartening to have to labor at making up for somebody else's blundering, when there is so much new work that needs to be done.

The condition shown by the landing-grid suspicions was a case in point. Blueskins were people who inherited a splotchy skin pigmentation from other people who'd survived a plague. Weald plainly maintained a one-planet quarantine against them. But a quarantine is normally an emergency measure. The Med Service should have taken over, wiped out the need for a quarantine, and then lifted it. It hadn't been done.

Calhoun fumed to himself.

The world of Weald Three grew brighter and brighter and became a disk. The disk had icecaps and a reasonable proportion of land and water surface. The ship decelerated, voices notifying observation from the surface, and the little ship came to a stop some five planetary diameters out from solidity. The landing field's force-field locked on to it, and its descent began.

The business of landing was all very familiar, from the blue rim which appeared at the limb of the planet from one diameter out, to the singular flowing-apart of the surface features as the ship sank still lower. There was the circular landing-grid, rearing skyward for nearly a mile. It could let down interstellar liners from emptiness and lift them out to emptiness again, with great convenience and economy for everyone.

It landed the Med Ship in its center, and there were officials to greet Calhoun, and he knew in advance the routine part of his visit. There would be an interview with the planet's chief executive, by whatever title he was called. There would be a banquet. Murgatroyd would be petted by everybody. There would be painful efforts to impress Calhoun with the splendid conduct of public health matters on Weald. He would be told much scandal.

He might find one man, somewhere, who passionately labored to advance the welfare of his fellow humans by finding out how to keep them well or, failing that, how to make them well when they got sick. And in two days, or three, Calhoun would be escorted back to the landing-grid, and lifted out to space, and he'd spend long empty days in overdrive and land somewhere else to do the whole thing all over again.

It all happened exactly as he expected, with one exception. Every human being he met on Weald wanted to talk about blueskins. Blueskins and the idea of blueskins obsessed everyone. Calhoun listened without asking questions until he had the picture of what blueskins meant to the people who talked of them. Then he knew there would be no use asking questions at random.

Nobody mentioned ever having seen a blueskin. Nobody mentioned a specific event in which a blueskin had at any named time taken part. But everybody was afraid of blueskins. It was a patterned, an inculcated, a stage-directed fixed idea. And it found expression in shocked references to the vileness, the depravity, the monstrousness of the blueskin inhabitants of Dara, from whom Weald must at all costs be protected.

It did not make sense. So Calhoun listened politely until he found an undistinguished medical man who wanted some special information about gene selection as practised halfway across the galaxy. He invited that man to the Med Ship, where he supplied the information not hitherto available. He saw his guest's eyes shine a little with that joyous awe a man feels when he finds out something he has wanted long and badly to know.

"Now," said Calhoun, "tell me something? Why does everybody on this planet hate the inhabitants of Dara? It's light-years away. Nobody claims to have suffered in person from them. Why make a point of hating them?"

The Wealdian doctor grimaced.

"They've blue patches on their skins. They're different from us. So they can be pictured as a danger and our political parties can make an election issue out of competing for the privilege of defending us from them. They had a plague on Dara, once. They're accused of still having it ready for export."

"Hm," said Calhoun. "The story is that they want to spread contagion here, eh? Doesn't anybody..." His tone was sardonic. "...doesn't anybody urge that they be massacred as an act of piety?"

"Yes-s-s," admitted the doctor reluctantly. "It's mentioned in political speeches."

"But how's it rationalized?" demanded Calhoun. "What's the argument to make pigment-patches involve moral and physical degradation, as I'm assured is the case?"

"In the public schools," said the doctor, "the children are taught that blueskins are now carriers of the disease they survived—three generations ago! That they hate everybody who isn't a blueskin. That they are constantly scheming to introduce their plague here so most of us will die and the rest will become blueskins. That's beyond rationalizing. It can't be true, but it's not safe to doubt it."

"Bad business," said Calhoun coldly. "That sort of thing usually costs lives in the end. It could lead to massacre!"

"Perhaps it has, in a way," said the doctor unhappily. "One doesn't like to think about it." He paused. "Twenty years ago there was a famine on Dara. There were crop failures. The situation must have been very bad: They built a spaceship.

"They've no use for such things normally, because no nearby planet will deal with them or let them land. But they built a spaceship and came here. They went in orbit around Weald. They asked to trade for shiploads of food. They offered any price in heavy metals—gold, platinum, irridium, and so on. They talked from orbit by vision communicators. They could be seen to be blueskins. You can guess what happened!"

"Tell me," said Calhoun.

"We armed ships in a hurry," admitted the doctor. "We chased their spaceship back to Dara. We hung in space off the planet. We told them we'd blast their world from pole to pole if they ever dared take to space again. We made them destroy their one ship, and we watched on visionscreens as it was done."

"But you gave them food?"

"No," said the doctor ashamedly. "They were blueskins."

"How bad was the famine?"

"Who knows? Any number may have starved! And we kept a squadron of armed ships in their skies for years—to keep them from spreading the plague, we said. And some of us believed it!"

The doctor's tone was purest irony.

"Lately," he said, "there's been a move for economy in our government. Simultaneously, we began to have a series of overabundant crops. The government had to buy the excess grain to keep the price up. Retired patrol ships, built to watch over Dara, were available for storage space. We filled them up with grain and sent them out into orbit. They're there now, hundreds of thousands or millions of tons of grain!"

"And Dara?"

The doctor shrugged. He stood up.

"Our hatred of Dara," he said, again ironically, "has produced one thing. Roughly halfway between here and Dara there's a two-planet solar system, Orede. There's a usable planet there. It was proposed to build an outpost of Weald there, against blueskins. Cattle were landed to run wild and multiply and make a reason for colonists to settle there.

"They did, but nobody wants to move near to blueskins! So Orede stayed uninhabited until a hunting party, shooting wild cattle, found an outcropping of heavy-metal ore. So now there's a mine there. And that's all. A few hundred men work the mine at fabulous wages. You may be asked to check on their health. But not Dara's!"

"I see," said Calhoun, frowning.

The doctor moved toward the Med Ship's exit port.

"I answered your questions," he said grimly. "But if I talked to anyone else as I've done to you, I'd be lucky only to be driven into exile!"

"I shan't give you away," said Calhoun. He did not smile.

When the doctor had gone, Calhoun said deliberately, "Murgatroyd, you should be grateful that you're a *tormal* and not a man. There's nothing about being a *tormal* to make you ashamed!"

Then he grimly changed his garments for the full-dress uniform of the Med Service. There was to be a banquet at which he would sit next to the planet's chief executive and hear innumerable speeches about the splendor of Weald. Calhoun had his own, strictly Med Service opinion of the planet's latest and most boasted-of achievement. It was a domed city in the polar regions, where nobody ever had to go outdoors.

He was less than professionally enthusiastic about the moving streets, and much less than approving of the dream broadcasts which supplied hypnotic, sleep-inducing rhythms to anybody who chose to listen to them. The price was that while asleep one would hear high praise of commercial products, and might believe them when awake.

But it was not Calhoun's function to criticize when it could be avoided. Med Service had been badly managed in Sector Twelve. So at the banquet Calhoun made a brief and diplomatic address in which he temperately praised what could be praised, and did not mention anything else.

The chief executive followed him. As head of the government he paid some tribute to the Med Service. But then he reminded his hearers proudly of the high culture, splendid health, and remarkable prosperity of the planet since his political party took office. This, he said, despite the need to be perpetually on guard against the greatest and most immediate danger to which any world in all the galaxy was exposed.

He referred to the blueskins, of course. He did not need to tell the people of Weald what vigilance, what constant watchfulness was necessary against that race of deprived and malevolent deviants from the norm of humanity. But Weald, he said with emotion, held aloft the torch of all that humanity held most dear, and defended not alone the lives of its people against blueskin contagion, but their noble heritage of ideals against blueskin pollution.

When he sat down, Calhoun said very politely, "It looks as if some day it should be practical politics to urge the massacre of all blueskins. Have you thought of that?"

The chief executive said comfortably, "The idea's been proposed. It's good politics to urge it, but it would be foolish to carry it out. People vote against blueskins. Wipe them out, and where'd you be?"

Calhoun ground his teeth—quietly.

There were more speeches. Then a messenger, white-faced, arrived with a written note for the chief executive. He read it and passed it to Calhoun. It was from the Ministry of Health. The spaceport reported that a ship had just broken out from overdrive within the Wealdian solar system. Its tape-transmitter had automatically signaled its arrival from the mining planet Orede.

But, having sent off its automatic signal, the ship lay dead in space. It did not drive toward Weald. It did not respond to signals. It drifted like a derelict upon no course at all. It seemed ominous, and since it came from Orede, the planet nearest to Dara of the blueskins, the health ministry informed the planet's chief executive.

"It'll be blueskins," said that astute person firmly. "They're next door to Orede. That's who's done this. It wouldn't surprise me if they'd seeded Orede with their plague, and this ship came from there to give us warning!"

"There's no evidence for anything of the sort," protested Calhoun. "A ship simply came out of overdrive and didn't signal further. That's all!"

"We'll see," said the chief executive ominously. "We'll go to the spaceport. There we'll get the news as it comes in, and can frame orders on the latest information."

He took Calhoun by the arm. Calhoun said sharply, "Murgatroyd!"

During the banquet, Murgatroyd had been visiting with the wives of the higher-up officials. They had enough of their husbands normally, without listening to their official speeches. Murgatroyd was brought, his small paunch distended with cakes and coffee and such delicacies as he'd been plied with. He was half comatose from overfeeding and overpetting, but he was glad to see Calhoun.

Calhoun held the little creature in his arms as the official groundcar raced through traffic with screaming sirens claiming the right of way. It reached the spaceport, where enormous metal girders formed a monster frame of metal lace against a star-filled sky. The chief executive strode magnificently into the spaceport offices. There was no news; the situation remained unchanged.

A ship from Orede had come out of overdrive and lay dead in emptiness. It did not answer calls. It did not move in space. It floated eerily in no orbit, going nowhere, doing nothing. And panic was the consequence.

It seemed to Calhoun that the official handling of the matter accounted for the terror that he could feel building up. The unexplained bit of news was on the air all over the planet Weald. There was nobody awake of all the world's population who did not believe that there was a new danger in the sky. Nobody doubted that it came from blueskins. The treatment of the news was precisely calculated to keep alive the hatred of Weald for the inhabitants of the world Dara.

Calhoun put Murgatroyd into the Med Ship and went back to the spaceport office. A small spaceboat, designed to inspect the circling grain ships from time to time, was already aloft. The landing-grid had thrust it swiftly out most of the way. Now it droned and drove on sturdily toward the enigmatic ship.

Calhoun took no part in the agitated conferences among the officials and news reporters at the spaceport. But he listened to the talk about him. As the investigating small ship drew nearer to the deathly-still cargo vessel, the guesses about the meaning of its breakout and following silence grew more and more wild.

But, singularly, there was no single suggestion that the mystery might not be the work of blueskins. Blueskins were scape-goats for all the fears and all the uneasiness a perhaps over-civilized world developed.

Presently the investigating spaceboat reached the mystery ship and circled it, beaming queries. No answer. It reported the cargo ship dark. No lights anywhere on or in it. There were no induction-surges from even pulsing, idling engines. Delicately, the messenger craft maneuvered until it touched the silent vessel. It reported that microphones detected no motion whatever inside.

"Let a volunteer go aboard," commanded the chief executive. "Let him report what he finds."

A pause. Then the solemn announcement of an intrepid volunteer's name, from far, far away. Calhoun listened, frowning darkly. This pompous heroism wouldn't be noticed in the Med Service. It would be routine behavior.

Suspenseful, second-by-second reports. The volunteer had rocketed himself across the emptiness between the two again separated ships. He had opened the airlock from outside. He'd gone in. He'd closed the outer airlock door. He'd opened the inner. He reported—

The relayed report was almost incoherent, what with horror and incredulity and the feeling of doom that came upon the volunteer. The ship was a bulk-cargo ore-carrier, designed to run between Orede and Weald with cargos of heavy-metal ores and a crew of no more than five men. There was no cargo in her holds now, though.

Instead, there were men. They packed the ship. They filled the corridors. They had crawled into every space where a man could find room to push himself. There were hundreds of them. It was insanity. And it had been greater insanity still for the ship to have taken off with so preposterous a load of living creatures.

But they weren't living any longer. The air apparatus had been designed for a crew of five. It would purify the air for possibly twenty or more. But there were hundreds of men in hiding as well as in plain view in the cargo ship from Orede. There were many, many times more than her air apparatus and reserve tanks could possibly have taken care of. They couldn't even have been fed during the journey from Orede to Weald.

But they hadn't starved. Air-scarcity killed them before the ship came out of overdrive.

A remarkable thing was that there was no written message in the ship's log which referred to its takeoff. There was no memorandum of the taking on of such an impossible number of passengers.

"The blueskins did it," said the chief executive of Weald. He was pale. All about Calhoun men looked sick and shocked and terrified. "It was the blueskins! We'll have to teach them a lesson!" Then he turned to Calhoun. "The volunteer who went on that ship—he'll have to stay there, won't he? He can't be brought back to Weald without bringing contagion."

Calhoun raged at him.

CHAPTER TWO

There was a certain coldness in the manner of those at the Weald spaceport when the Med Ship left next morning. Calhoun was not popular because Weald was scared. It had been conditioned to scare easily, where blueskins might be involved. Its children were trained to react explosively when the word *blueskin* was uttered in their hearing, and its adults tended to say it when anything causing uneasiness entered their minds. So a planet-wide habit of irrational response had formed and was not seen to be irrational because almost everybody had it.

The volunteer who'd discovered the tragedy on the ship from Orede was safe, though. He'd made a completely conscientious survey of the ship he'd volunteered to enter and examine. For his courage, he'd have been doomed but for Calhoun.

The reaction of his fellow citizens was that by entering the ship he might have become contaminated by blueskin infectious material of the plague still existed, and *if* the men in the ship had caught it (but they certainly hadn't died of it), and *if* there had been blueskins on Orede to communicate it (for which there was no evidence), and *if* blueskins were responsible for the tragedy. Which was at the moment pure supposition. But Weald feared he might bring death back to Weald if he were allowed to return.

Calhoun saved his life. He ordered that the guardship admit him to its airlock, which then was to be filled with steam and chlorine. The combination would sterilize and even partly eat away his spacesuit, after which the chlorine and steam should be bled out to space, and air from the ship let into the lock.

If he stripped off the spacesuit without touching its outer surface, and reentered the investigating ship while the suit was flung outside by a man in another spacesuit, handling it with a pole he'd fling after it, there could be no possible contamination brought back.

Calhoun was quite right, but Weald in general considered that he'd persuaded the government to take an unreasonable risk.

There were other reasons for disapproving of him. Calhoun had been unpleasantly frank. The coming of the death-ship stirred to frenzy those people who believed that all blueskins should be exterminated as a pious act. They'd appeared on every vision screen, citing not only the ship from Orede but other incidents which they interpreted as crimes against Weald.

They demanded that all Wealdian atomic reactors be modified to turn out fusion-bomb materials while a space fleet was made ready for an anti-blueskin crusade. They confidently demanded such a rain of fusion bombs on Dara that no blueskin, no animal, no shred of vegetation, no fish in the deepest ocean, not even a living virus particle of the blueskin plague could remain alive on the blueskin world.

One of these vehement orators even asserted that Calhoun agreed that no other course was possible, speaking for the Interstellar Medical Service. And Calhoun furiously demanded a chance to deny it by broadcast, and he made a bitter and indiscreet speech from which a planet-wide audience inferred that he thought them fools.

He did.

So he was definitely unpopular when his ship lifted from Weald. He'd curtly given his destination as Orede, from which the death-ship had come. The landing-grid locked on, raised the small spacecraft until Weald was a great shining ball below it, and then somehow scornfully cast him off. The Med Ship was free, in clear space where there was not enough of a gravitational field to hinder overdrive.

He aimed for his destination, his face very grim. He said savagely, "Get set, Murgatroyd! Overdrive coming!"

He thumbed down the overdrive button. The universe of stars went out, while everything living in the ship felt the customary sensations of dizziness, of nausea, and of a spiraling fall to nothingness. Then there was silence.

The Med Ship actually moved at a rate which was a preposterous number of times the speed of light, but it felt absolutely solid, absolutely firm and fixed. A ship in overdrive feels exactly as if it were buried deep in the core of a planet. There is no vibration. There is no sign of anything but solidity and, if one looks out a port, there is only utter blackness plus an absence of sound fit to make one's eardrums crack.

But within seconds random tiny noises began. There was a reel and there were sound-speakers to keep the ship from sounding like a grave. The reel played and the speakers gave off minute creakings, and meaningless hums, and very tiny noises of every imaginable sort, all of which were just above the threshold of the inaudible.

Calhoun fretted. Sector Twelve was in very bad shape. A conscientious Med Service man would never have let the anti-blueskin obsession go unmentioned in a report on Weald. Health is not only a physical affair. There is mental health, also. When mental health goes a civilization can be destroyed more surely and more terribly than by any imaginable war or plague germs. A plague kills off those who are susceptible to it, leaving immunes to build up a world again. But immunes are the first to be killed when a mass neurosis sweeps a population.

Weald was definitely a Med Service problem world. Dara was another. And when hundreds of men jammed themselves into a cargo spaceship which could not furnish them with air to breathe, and took off and went into overdrive before the air could fail… Orede called for no less of worry.

"I think," said Calhoun dourly, "that I'll have some coffee."

Coffee was one of the words that Murgatroyd recognized. Ordinarily he stirred immediately on hearing it, and watched the coffeemaker with bright, interested eyes. He'd even tried to imitate Calhoun's motions with it, once, and had scorched his paws in the attempt. But this time he did not move.

Calhoun turned his head. Murgatroyd sat on the floor, his long tail coiled reflectively about a chair leg. He watched the door of the Med Ship's sleeping cabin.

"Murgatroyd," said Calhoun. "I mentioned coffee!"

"*Chee!*" shrilled Murgatroyd.

But he continued to look at the door. The temperature was kept lower in the other cabin, and the look of things was different than the control compartment. The difference was part of the means by which a man was able to be alone for weeks on end—alone save for his *tormal*—without becoming ship-happy.

There were other carefully thought out items in the ship with the same purpose. But none of them should cause

Murgatroyd to stare fixedly and fascinatedly at the sleeping cabin door. Not when coffee was in the making!

Calhoun considered. He became angry at the immediate suspicion that occurred to him. As a Med Service man, he was duty-bound to be impartial. To be impartial might mean not to side absolutely with Weald in its enmity to blueskins.

And the people of Weald had refused to help Dara in a time of famine, and had blockaded that pariah world for years afterward. And they had other reasons for hating the people they'd treated badly. It was entirely reasonable for some fanatic on Weald to consider that Calhoun must be killed lest he be of help to the blueskins Weald abhorred.

In fact, it was quite possible that somebody had stowed away on the Med Ship to murder Calhoun, so that there would be no danger of any report favorable to Dara ever being presented anywhere. If so, such a stowaway would be in the sleeping cabin now, waiting for Calhoun to walk in unsuspiciously, only to be shot dead.

So Calhoun made coffee. He slipped a blaster into a pocket where it would be handy. He filled a small cup for Murgatroyd and a large one for himself, and then a second large one.

He tapped on the sleeping cabin door, standing aside lest a blaster-bolt come through it.

"Coffee's ready," he said sardonically. "Come out and join us."

There was a long pause. Calhoun rapped again.

"You've a seat at the captain's table," he said more sardonically still. "It's not polite to keep me waiting!"

He listened, alert for a rush which would be a fanatic's desperate attempt to do murder despite premature discovery. He was prepared to shoot quite ruthlessly, because he was on duty and the Med Service did not approve of the extermination of populations, however justified another population might consider it.

But there was no rush. Instead, there came hesitant foot-falls whose sound made Calhoun start. The door of the cabin slid slowly aside. A girl appeared in the opening, desperately white and desperately composed.

"H-how did you know I was there?" she asked shakily. She moistened her lips. "You didn't see me! I was in a closet, and you didn't even enter the room!"

Calhoun said grimly, "I've sources of information. Murgatroyd told me this time. May I present him? Murgatroyd, our passenger. Shake hands."

Murgatroyd moved forward, stood on his hind legs and offered a skinny, furry paw. She did not move. She stared at Calhoun.

"Better shake hands," said Calhoun, as grimly as before. "It might relax the tension a little. And do you want to tell me your story? You have one ready, I'm sure."

The girl swallowed. Murgatroyd shook hands gravely. He said, "*Chee-chee!*" in the shrillest of trebles and went back to his former position.

"The story?" said Calhoun insistently.

"There—there isn't any," said the girl unsteadily. "Just that I—I need to get to Orede, and you're going there. There's no other way to go, now."

"To the contrary," said Calhoun. "There'll undoubtedly be a fleet heading for Orede as soon as it can be assembled and armed. But I'm afraid that as a story yours isn't good enough. Try another."

She shivered a little.

"I'm running away…"

"Ah!" said Calhoun. "In that case I'll take you back."

"No!" she said fiercely. "I'll—I'll die first! I'll wreck this ship first!"

Her hand came from behind her. There was a tiny blaster in it. But it shook visibly as she tried to aim it.

"I'll shoot out the controls!"

Calhoun blinked. He'd had to make a drastic change in his estimate of the situation the instant he saw that the stowaway was a girl. Now he had to make another when her threat was not to kill him but to disable the ship. Women are rarely assassins, and when they are they don't use energy weapons. Daggers and poisons are more typical. But this girl threatened to destroy the ship rather than its owner, so she was not actually an assassin at all.

"I'd rather you didn't do that," said Calhoun dryly. "Besides, you'd get deadly bored if we were stuck in a derelict waiting for our air and food to give out."

Murgatroyd, for no reason whatever, felt it necessary to enter the conversation:

"*Chee-chee-chee!*"

"A very sensible suggestion," observed Calhoun. "We'll sit down and have a cup of coffee." To the girl he said, "I'll take you to Orede, since that's where you say you want to go."

"I have a sweetheart there…"

Calhoun shook his head.

"No," he said reprovingly. "Nearly all the mining colony had packed itself into the ship that came into Weald with everybody dead. But not all. And there's been no check of what men were in the ship and what men weren't. You wouldn't go to Orede if it were likely your sweetheart had died on the way to you. Here's your coffee. Sugar or saccho, and do you take cream?"

She trembled a little, but she took the cup.

"I don't understand."

"Murgatroyd and I..." explained Calhoun—and he did not know whether he spoke out of anger or something else. "...we are do-gooders. We go around trying to keep people from getting sick or dying. Sometimes we even try to keep them from getting killed. It's our profession. We practise it even on our own behalf. We want to stay alive. So since you make such drastic threats, we will take you where you want to go. Especially since we're going there anyhow."

"You don't believe anything I've said!" It was a statement.

"Not a word," admitted Calhoun. "But you'll probably tell us something more believable presently. When did you eat last?"

"Yesterday."

"Would you rather do your own cooking?" asked Calhoun politely. "Or would you permit me to ready a snack?"

"I—I'll do it," she said.

She drank her coffee first, however, and then Calhoun showed her how to punch the readier for such-and-such dishes, to be extracted from storage and warmed or chilled, as the case might be, and served at dialed-for intervals. There was also equipment for preparing food for oneself, in one's own chosen manner—again an item to help make solitude not unendurable.

Calhoun deliberately immersed himself in the Galactic Directory, looking up the planet Orede. He was headed there, but he'd had no reason to inform himself about it before. Now he read with every appearance of absorption.

The girl ate daintily. Murgatroyd watched with highly amiable interest. But she looked acutely uncomfortable.

Calhoun finished with the Directory. He got out the micro-film reels which contained more information. He was specifically after the Med Service history of all the planets in this sector. He went through the filmed record of every inspection ever made on Weald and on Dara.

But Sector Twelve had not been run well. There was no adequate account of a plague which had wiped out three-quarters of the population of an inhabited planet! It had happened shortly after one Med Ship visit, and was over before another Med Ship came by.

There should have been a painstaking investigation, even after the fact. There should have been a collection of infectious material and a reasonably complete identification and study of the agent. It hadn't been made. There was probably some other emergency at the time, and it slipped by. Calhoun, whose career was not to be spent in this sector, resolved on a blistering report about this negligence and its consequences.

He kept himself casually busy, ignoring the girl. A Med Ship man has resources of study and meditation with which to occupy himself during overdrive travel from one planet to another. Calhoun made use of those resources. He acted as if he were completely unconscious of the stowaway. But Murgatroyd watched her with charmed attention.

Hours after her discovery, she said uneasily, "Please?"

Calhoun looked up.

"Yes?"

"I don't know exactly how things stand."

"You are a stowaway," said Calhoun. "Legally, I have the right to put you out the airlock. It doesn't seem necessary. There's a cabin. When you're sleepy, use it. Murgatroyd and I can make out quite well out here. When you're hungry, you now know how to get something to eat. When we land on Orede, you'll probably go about whatever business you have there. That's all."

She stared at him.

"But you don't believe what I've told you!"

"No," agreed Calhoun, but didn't add to the statement.

"But—I will tell you," she offered. "The police were after me. I had to get away from Weald! I had to! I'd stolen—"

He shook his head.

"No," he said. "If you were a thief, you'd say anything in the world except that you were a thief. You're not ready to tell the truth yet. You don't have to, so why tell me anything? I suggest that you get some sleep. Incidentally, there's no lock on the cabin door because there's only supposed to be one person on this ship at a time. But you can brace a chair to fasten it somehow or other. Good night."

She rose slowly. Twice her lips parted as if to speak again, but then she went into the other cabin and closed herself in. There was the sound of a chair being wedged against the door.

Murgatroyd blinked at the place where she'd disappeared and then climbed up into Calhoun's lap, with complete assurance of welcome. He settled himself and was silent for moments. Then he said, "*Chee!*"

"I believe you're right," said Calhoun. "She doesn't belong on Weald, or with the conditioning she'd have had, there'd be only one place she'd dread worse than Orede, which would be Dara. But I doubt she'd be afraid to land even on Dara."

Murgatroyd liked to be talked to. He liked to pretend that he carried on a conversation, like humans.

"*Chee-chee!*" he said with conviction.

"Definitely," agreed Calhoun. "She's not doing this for her personal advantage. Whatever she thinks she'd doing, it's more important to her than her own life. Murgatroyd…"

"*Chee?*" said Murgatroyd in an inquiring tone.

"There are wild cattle on Orede," said Calhoun. "Herds and herds of them. I have a suspicion that somebody's been shooting them. Lots of them. Do you agree? Don't you think that a lot of cattle have been slaughtered on Orede lately?"

Murgatroyd yawned. He settled himself still more comfortably in Calhoun's lap.

"*Chee*," he said drowsily.

He went to sleep, while Calhoun continued the examination of highly condensed information. Presently he looked up the normal rate of increase, with other data, among herds of *bovis domesticus* in a wild state, on planets where there are no natural enemies.

It wasn't unheard-of for a world to be stocked with useful types of Terran fauna and flora before it was attempted to be colonized. Terran life-forms could play the devil with alien ecological systems—very much to humanity's benefit. Familiar microorganisms and a standard vegetation added to the practicality of human settlements on otherwise alien worlds. But sometimes the results were strange.

They weren't often so strange, however, as to cause some hundreds of men to pack themselves frantically aboard a cargo ship which couldn't possibly sustain them, so that every man must die while the ship was in overdrive.

Still, by the time Calhoun turned in on a spare pneumatic mattress, he had calculated that as few as a dozen head of cattle, turned loose on a suitable planet, would have increased to herds of thousands or tens or even hundreds of thousands in much less time than had probably elapsed.

The Med Ship drove on in seemingly absolute solidity, with no sound from without, with no sight to be seen outside, with no evidence at all that it was not buried in the heart of a planet instead of flashing through emptiness at a speed so great as to have no meaning.

Next ship-day the girl looked oddly at Calhoun when she appeared in the control room. Murgatroyd regarded her with great interest. Calhoun nodded politely and went back to what he'd been doing before she appeared.

"Shall I have breakfast?" she asked uncertainly.

"Murgatroyd and I have," he told her. "Why not?"

Silently, she operated the food-readier. She ate. Calhoun gave a very good portrayal of a man who will respond politely when spoken to, but who was busy with activities remote from stowaways.

About noon, ship-time, she asked, "When will we get to Orede?"

Calhoun told her absently, as if he were thinking of something else.

"What—what do you think happened there? I mean, to make that tragedy in the ship."

"I don't know," said Calhoun. "But I disagree with the authorities on Weald. I don't think it was a planned atrocity of the blueskins."

"Wh-what are blueskins?" asked the girl.

Calhoun turned around and looked at her directly.

"When lying," he said mildly, "you tell as much by what you pretend isn't, as by what you pretend is. You know what blueskins are!"

"But what do you think they are?" she asked.

"There used to be a human disease called smallpox," said Calhoun. "When people recovered from it, they were usually marked. Their skin had little scar pits here and there. At one time, back on Earth, it was expected that everybody would catch smallpox sooner or later, and a large percentage would die of it.

"And it was so much a matter of course that if they printed a picture of a criminal they never mentioned it if he were pock-marked. It was no distinction. But if he didn't have the markings, they'd mention that!" He paused. "Those pock-marks weren't hereditary, but otherwise a blueskin is like a man who had them. He can't be anything else!"

"Then you think they're human?"

"There's never yet been a case of reverse evolution," said Calhoun. "Maybe Pithecanthropus had a monkey uncle, but no Pithecanthropus ever went monkey."

She turned abruptly away. But she glanced at him often during that day. He continued to busy himself with those activities which make Med Ship life consistent with retained sanity.

Next day she asked without preliminary, "Don't you believe the blueskins planned for the ship with the dead men to arrive at Weald and spread plague there?"

"No," said Calhoun.

"Why?"

"It couldn't possibly work," Calhoun told her. "With only dead men on board, the ship wouldn't arrive at a place where the landing-grid could bring it down. So that would be no good. And plague-stricken living men wouldn't try to conceal that they had the plague. They might ask for help, but they'd know they'd instantly be killed on Weald if they were found to be plague victims. So that would be no good, either! No, the ship wasn't intended to land plague on Weald."

"Are you friendly to blueskins?" she asked uncertainly.

"Within reason," said Calhoun, "I am a well-wisher to all the human race. You're slipping, though. When using the word *blueskin* you should say it uncomfortably, as if it were a word no refined person liked to pronounce. You don't. We'll land on Orede tomorrow, by the way. If you ever intend to tell me the truth, there's not much time left."

She bit her lips. Twice, during the remainder of the day, she faced him and opened her mouth as if to speak, and then turned away again. Calhoun shrugged. He had fairly definite ideas about her, by now. He carefully kept them tentative, but no girl born and raised on Weald would willingly go to Orede, with all of Weald believing that a shipload of miners preferred death to remaining there. It tied in, like everything else that was unpleasant, to blueskins. Nobody from Weald would dream of landing on Orede! Not now!

A little before the Med Ship was due to break out from overdrive, the girl said very carefully, "You've been very kind. I'd like to thank you. I—I didn't really believe I would live to get to Orede."

Calhoun raised his eyebrows.

"I wish I could tell you everything you want to know," she added regretfully. "I think you're...really decent. But some thing..."

Calhoun said caustically, "You've told me a great deal. You weren't born on Weald. You weren't raised there. The people of Dara—notice that I don't say blueskins, though they are—the people of Dara have made at least one space ship since Weald threatened them with extermination. There is probably a new food shortage on Dara now, leading to pure desperation. Most likely it's bad enough to make them risk landing on Orede to kill cattle and freeze beef to help. They've worked out—"

She gasped and sprang to her feet. She snatched out the tiny blaster in her pocket. She pointed it waveringly at him.

"I have to kill you!" she cried desperately. "I—I have to!"

Calhoun reached out. She tugged despairingly at the blaster's trigger. Nothing happened. Before she could realize that she hadn't turned off the safety, Calhoun twisted the weapon from her fingers. He stepped back.

"Good girl!" he said approvingly. "I'll give this back to you when we land. And thanks. Thanks very much!"

She wrung her hands. Then she stared at him.

"Thanks? When I tried to kill you?"

"Of course!" said Calhoun. "I'd made guesses. I couldn't know that they were right. When you tried to kill me, you confirmed every one. Now, when we land on Orede I'm going to get you to try to put me in touch with your friends. It's going to be tricky, because they must be pretty well scared about that ship. But it's a highly desirable thing to get done!"

He went to the ships' control board and sat down before it.

"Twenty minutes to breakhour," he observed.

Murgatroyd peered out of his little cubbyhole. His eyes were anxious. *Tormals* are amiable little creatures. During the days in overdrive, Calhoun had paid less than the usual amount of attention to Murgatroyd, while the girl was fascinating.

They'd made friends, awkwardly on the girl's part, very pleasantly on Murgatroyd's. But only moments ago there had been bitter emotion in the air. Murgatroyd had fled to his cubbyhole to escape it. He was distressed. Now that there was silence again, he peered out unhappily.

"*Chee?*" he queried plaintively. "*Chee-chee-chee?*"

Calhoun said matter-of-factly, "It's all right, Murgatroyd. If we aren't blasted as we try to land, we should be able to make friends with everybody and get something accomplished."

The statement was hopelessly inaccurate.

CHAPTER THREE

There was no answer from the ground when breakout came and Calhoun drove the Med Ship to a favourable position for a call. He patiently repeated, over and over again, that the Med Ship *Aesclipus Twenty* notified its arrival and requested coordinates for landing. He added that its mass was fifty standard tons and that the purpose of its visit was a planetary health inspection.

But there was no reply. There should have been a crisp description of the direction from the planet's center at which, a certain time so many hours or minutes later, the force-fields of the grid would find it convenient to lock onto and lower the Med Ship. But the communicator remained silent.

"There is a landing-grid," said Calhoun, frowning, "and if they're using it to load fresh meat for Dara, from the herds I'm told about, it should be manned. But they don't seem to intend to answer. Maybe they think that if they pretend I'm not here I'll go away."

He reflected, and his frown deepened.

"If I didn't know what I know, I might. So if I land on emergency rockets the blueskins down below may decide that I come from Weald. And in that case it would be reasonable to blast me before I could land and unload some fighting men. On the other hand, no ship from Weald would conceivably land without impassioned assurance that it was safe. It would drop bombs." He turned to the girl. "How many Darians down below?"

She shook her head.

"You don't know," said Calhoun, "or won't tell, yet. But they ought to be told about the arrival of that ship at Weald, and what Weald thinks about it! My guess is that you came to tell them. It isn't likely that Dara gets news directly from Weald. Where were you put ashore from Dara, when you set out to be a spy?"

Her lips parted to speak, but she compressed them tightly. She shook her head again.

"It must have been plenty far away," said Calhoun restlessly. "Your people would have built a ship, and made fine forged papers for it, and they'd travel so far from this part of space that when they landed nobody would think of Dara. They'd use make-up to cover the blue spots, but maybe it was so far away that blueskins had never been heard of!"

Her face looked pinched, but she did not reply.

"Then they'd land half a dozen of you, with a supply of make-up for the blue patches. And you'd separate, and take ships that went various roundabout ways, and arrive on Weald one by one, to see what could be done there to—" He stopped. "When did you find out positively that there wasn't any plague any more?"

She began to grow pale.

"I'm not a mind reader," said Calhoun. "But it adds up. You're from Dara. You've been on Weald. It's practically certain that there are other...agents, if you like that word better, on Weald. And there hasn't been a plague on Weald so you people aren't carriers of it. But you knew it in advance, I think. How'd you learn? Did a ship in some sort of trouble land there, on Dara?"

"Y—yes," said the girl. "We wouldn't let it go again. But the people didn't catch—they didn't die. They lived—"

She stopped short.

"It's not fair to trap me!" she cried passionately. "It's not fair!"

"I'll stop," said Calhoun.

He turned to the control board. The Med Ship was only planetary diameters from Orede, now, and the electron telescope showed shining stars in leisurely motion across its screen. Then a huge, gibbous shining shape appeared, and there were irregular patches of that muddy color which is seabottom, and varicolored areas which were plains and forests. Also there were mountains. Calhoun steadied the image, and squinted at it.

"The mine," he observed, "was found by members of a hunting party, killing wild cattle for sport."

Even a small planet has many millions of square miles of surface, and a single human installation on a whole world will not be easy to find by random search. But there were clues to this one. Men hunting for sport would not choose a tropic nor an arctic climate to hunt in. So if they found a mineral deposit, it would have been in a temperate zone.

Cattle would not be found deep in a mountainous terrain. The mine would not be on a prairie. The settlement on Orede, then, would be near the edge of mountains, not far from a prairie such as wild cattle would frequent, and it would be in a temperate climate.

Forested areas could be ruled out. And there would be a landing-grid. Handling only one ship at a time, it might be a very small grid. It could be only hundreds of yards across and less than half a mile high. But its shadow would be distinctive.

Calhoun searched among low mountains near unforested prairie in a temperate zone. He found a speck.

He enlarged it manyfold. It was the mine on Orede. There were heaps of tailings. There was something which cast a long, lacy shadow: the landing-grid.

"But they don't answer our call," observed Calhoun, "so we go down unwelcomed."

He inverted the Med Ship and the emergency rockets boomed. The ship plunged planetward.

A long time later it was deep in the planet's atmosphere. The noise of its rockets had become thunderous, with air to carry and to reinforce the sound.

"Hold on to something, Murgatroyd," commanded Calhoun. "We may have to dodge some ack."

But nothing came up from below. The Med Ship again inverted itself, and its rockets pointed toward the planet and poured out pencil-thin, blue-white, high-velocity flames. It checked slightly, but continued to descend. It was not directly above the grid.

It swept downward until almost level with the peaks of the mountains in which the mine lay. It tilted again, and swept onward over the mountaintops, and then tilted once more and went racing up the valley in which the landing-grid was plainly visible. Calhoun swung it on an erratic course, lest there be opposition.

But there was no sign. Then the rockets bellowed, and the ship slowed its forward motion, hovered momentarily, and settled to solidity outside the framework of the grid. The grid was small, as Calhoun reasoned. But it reached interminably toward the sky.

The rockets cut off. Slender as the flames had been, they'd melted and bored thin drill-holes deep into the soil. Molten rock boiled and bubbled down below. But there seemed no other sound. There was no other motion. There was absolute stillness all around. But when Calhoun switched on the outside microphones a faint, sweet melange of high-pitched chirpings came from tiny creatures hidden under the vegetation of the mountainsides.

Calhoun put a blaster in his pocket and stood up.

"We'll see what it looks like outside," he said with a certain grimness. "I don't quite believe what the vision screens show."

Minutes later he stepped down to the ground from the Med Ship's exit port. The ship had landed perhaps a hundred feet from what once had been a wooden building. In it, ore from the mines was concentrated and the useless tailings carried away by a conveyer belt to make a monstrous pile of broken stone. But there was no longer a building.

Next to it there had been a structure containing an ore-crusher. The massive machinery could still be seen, but the structure was in fragments. Next to that, again, had been the shaft-head shelters of the mine. They also were shattered practically to matchsticks.

The look of the ground about the building sites was simply and purely impossible. It was a mass of hoofprints. Cattle by thousands and tens of thousands had trampled everything. Cattle had burst in the wooden sides of the buildings. Cattle had piled themselves up against the beams upholding roofs until the buildings collapsed.

Then cattle had gone plunging over the wrecked buildings until there was nothing left but indescribable chaos. Many, many cattle had died in the crush. There were heaps of dead beasts about the metal girders which were the foundation of the landing-grid. The air was tainted by the smell of carrion.

The settlement had been destroyed, positively by stampeded cattle in tens or hundreds of thousands charging blindly through and over and upon it. Senselessly, they'd trampled each other to horrible shapelessness. The mine shaft was not choked, because enormously strong timbers had fallen across and blocked it. But everything else was pure destruction.

Calhoun said evenly, "Clever! Very clever! You can't blame men when beasts stampede. We should accept the evidence that some monstrous herd, making its way through a mountain pass, somehow went crazy and bolted for the plains. This settlement got in the way and it was too bad for the settlement! Everything's explained, except the ship that went to Weald.

"A cattle stampede, yes. Anybody can believe that! But there was a man stampede. Men stampeded into the ship as blindly as the cattle trampled down this little town. The ship stampeded off into space as insanely as the cattle. But a stampede of men and cattle, in the same place? That's a little too much!"

"But what—"

"How," asked Calhoun directly, "do you intend to get in touch with your friends here?"

"I—I don't know," she said, distressed. "But if the ship stays here, they're bound to come and see why. Won't they? Or will they?"

"If they're sane, they won't," said Calhoun. "The one undesirable thing, here, would be human footprints on top of cattle tracks. If your friends are a meat-getting party from Dara, as I believe, they should cover up their tracks, get off-planet as fast as possible, and pray that no signs of their former presence are ever discovered. That would be their best first move, certainly!"

"What should I do?" she asked helplessly.

"I'm far from sure. At a guess, and for the moment, probably nothing. I'll work something out. I've got the devil of a job before me, though. I can't spend but so much time here."

"You can leave me here…"

He grunted and turned away. It was naturally unthinkable that he should leave another human being on a supposedly uninhabited planet, with the knowledge that it might actually be uninhabited, and the future knowledge that any visitors would have the strongest of possible reasons to hide themselves away.

He believed that there were Darians here, and the girl in the Med ship, so he also believed, was also a Darian. But any who might be hiding had so much to lose if they were discovered that they might be hundreds or even thousands of miles from anywhere a space ship would normally land—if they hadn't fled after the incident of the spaceship's departure with its load of doomed passengers.

Considered detachedly, the odds were that there was again a food shortage on Dara; that blueskins, in desperation, had raided or were raiding or would raid the cattle herds of Orede for food to carry back to their home planet; that somehow the miners on Orede had found that they had blueskin neighbors, and died of the consequences of their terror. It was a risky guess to make on such evidence as Calhoun considered he had, but no other guess was possible.

If his guess were right, he was under some obligation to do exactly what he believed the girl considered her mission—to warn all blueskins that Weald would presently try to find them on Orede, when all hell must break loose upon Dara for punishment. But if there were men here, he couldn't leave a written warning for them in default of friendly contact.

They might not find it, and a search party of Wealdians might. All he could possibly do was try to make contact and give warning by such means as would leave no evidence behind that he'd done so. Weald would consider a warning sure proof of blueskin guilt.

It was not satisfactory to be limited to broadcasts which might or might not be picked up, and were unlikely to be acknowledged. But he settled down with the communicator to make the attempt.

He called first on a GC wave length and form. It was unlikely that blueskins would use general communication bands to keep in touch with each other, but it had to be tried. He broadcast, tuned as broadly as possible, and went up and down the GC spectrum, repeating his warning painstakingly and listening without hope for a reply.

He did find one spot on the dial where there was re-radiation of his message, as if from a tuned receiver. But he could not get a fix on it: nobody might be listening. He exhausted the normal communication pattern. Then he broadcast on old-fashioned amplitude modulation which a modern communicator would not pick up at all, and which therefore might be used by men in hiding.

He worked for a long time. Then he shrugged and gave it up. He'd repeated to absolute tedium the facts that any Darians—blueskins—on Orede ought to know. There'd been no answer. And it was all too likely that if he'd been received, that those who heard him took his message for a trick to discover if there were any hearers.

He clicked off at last and stood up, shaking his head. Suddenly the Med Ship seemed empty. Then he saw Murgatroyd staring vexedly at the exit port. The inner door of that small airlock was closed. The telltale light said the outer door was not locked. Someone had gone out quietly. The girl. Of course.

Calhoun said angrily, "How long ago, Murgatroyd?"

"*Chee!*" said Murgatroyd indignantly.

It wasn't an answer, but it showed that Murgatroyd was vexed that he'd been left behind. He and the girl were close friends, now. If she'd left Murgatroyd in the ship when he wanted to go with her, then she wasn't coming back.

Calhoun swore. He made certain she was not in the ship. He flipped the outside-speaker switch and said curtly into the microphone, "Coffee! Murgatroyd and I are having coffee. Will you come back, please?"

He repeated the call, and repeated it again. Multiplied as his voice was by the speakers, she should hear him within a mile. She did not appear. He went to a small and inconspicuous closet and armed himself. A Med Ship man was not ever expected to fight, but there were blast-rifles available for extreme emergency.

When he'd slung a power-pack over his shoulder and reached the airlock, there was still no sign of his late stowaway. He stood in the airlock door for long minutes, staring angrily about. Almost certainly she wouldn't be looking in the mountains for men of Dara come here for cattle. He used a pair of binoculars, first at low-magnification to search as wide an area down-valley as possible, and then at highest power to search the most likely routes.

He found a small, bobbing speck beyond a faraway hill crest. It was her head. It went down below the hilltop.

He snapped a command to Murgatroyd, and when the *tormal* was on the ground outside, he locked the port with that combination that nobody but a Med Ship man was at all likely to discover or use.

"She's an idiot!" he told Murgatroyd sourly. "Come along! We've got to be idiots too!"

He set out in pursuit.

There was blue sky overhead, as was inevitable on any oxygen-atmosphere planet of a Sol-type yellow sun. There were mountains, as is universal in planets whose surface rises and falls and folds and bends from the effects of weather or vulcanism. There were plants, as has come about wherever microorganisms have broken down rock to a state where it can nourish vegetation. And naturally there were animals.

There were even trees of severely practical design, and underbrush and ground-cover equivalent to grass. There was, in short, a perfectly predictable ecological system on Orede. The organic molecules involved in life here would be made up of the same elements in the same combinations as elsewhere where the same conditions of temperature and moisture and sunshine obtained.

It was a distinctly Earthlike world, as it could not help but be, and it was reasonable for cattle to thrive and increase here. Only men's minds kept it from being a place where humans would thrive, too.

But only Calhoun would have considered the splintered settlement a proof of that last.

The girl had a long start. Twice Calhoun came to places where she could have chosen either of two ways onward. Each time he had to determine which she'd followed. That cost time. Then the mountains abruptly ended and a vast undulating plain stretched away to the horizon. There were at least two large masses and many smaller clumps of what could only be animals gathered together. Cattle.

But here the girl was plainly in view. Calhoun increased his stride. He began to gain on her. She did not look behind.

Murgatroyd said *"Chee!"* in a complaining tone.

"I should have left you behind," agreed Calhoun dourly, "but there was and is a chance I won't get back. You'll have to keep on hiking."

He plodded on. His memory of the terrain around the mining settlement told him that there was no definite destination in the girl's mind. But she was in no such despair as to want deliberately to be lost. She'd guessed, Calhoun believed, that if there were Darians on the planet, they'd keep the landing-grid under observation.

If they saw her leave that area and could see that she was alone, they should intercept her to find out the meaning of the Med Ship's landing. Then she could identify herself as one of them and give them the terribly necessary warning of Weald's suspicions.

"But," said Calhoun sourly, "if she's right, they'll have seen me marching after her now, which spoils her scheme. And I'd like to help it, but the way she's going is too dangerous!"

He went down into one of the hollows of the uneven plain. He saw a clump of a dozen or so cattle a little distance away. The bull looked up and snorted. The cows regarded him truculently. Their air was not one of bovine tranquility.

He was up the farther hillside and out of sight before the bull worked himself up to a charge. Then Calhoun suddenly remembered one of the items in the data about cattle he'd looked into just the other day. He felt himself grow pale.

"Murgatroyd!" he said sharply. "We've got to catch up! Fast! Stay with me if you can, but..." He was jog-trotting as he spoke. "...even if you get lost I have to hurry!"

He ran fifty paces and walked fifty paces. He ran fifty and walked fifty. He saw her, atop a rolling of the ground. She came to a full stop. He ran. He saw her turn to retrace her steps. He flung off the safety of the blast-rifle and let off a roaring blast at the ground for her to hear.

Suddenly she was fleeing desperately, toward him. He plunged on. She vanished down into a hollow. Horns appeared over the hillcrest she'd just left. Cattle appeared. Four, a dozen fifteen, twenty! They moved ominously in her wake.

He saw her again, running frantically over another upward swell of the prairie. He let off another blast to guide her. He ran on at top speed with Murgatroyd trailing anxiously behind. From time to time Murgatroyd called *"Chee-chee-chee!"* in frightened pleading not to be abandoned.

More cattle appeared against the horizon. Fifty or a hundred. They came after the first clump. The first group of a bull and his harem were moving faster, now. The girl fled from them, but it is the instinct of beef-cattle on the open range—Calhoun had learned it only two days before—to charge any human they find on foot. A mounted man to their dim minds is a creature to be tolerated or fled from, but a human on foot is to be crushed and stamped and gored.

Those in the lead were definitely charging now, with heads bent low. The bull charged furiously with shut eyes, as bulls do, but the cows, many times more deadly, charged with their eyes wide open and wickedly alert, and with a lumbering speed much greater than the girl could manage.

She came up over the last rise, chalky-white and gasping, her hair flying, in the last extremity of terror. The nearest of the pursuing cattle were within ten yards when Calhoun fired from twenty yards beyond. One creature bellowed as the blast-bolt struck.

It went down and others crashed into it and swept over it, and more came on. The girl saw Calhoun now, and ran toward him, panting. He knelt very deliberately and began to check the charge by shooting the leading animals.

He did not succeed. There were more cattle following the first, and more and more behind them. It appeared that all the cattle on the plain joined in the blind and senseless charge. The thudding of hoofs became a mutter and then a rumble and then a growl.

Plunging, clumsy figures rushed past on either side. But horns and heads heaved up over the mound of animals Calhoun had shot. He shot them too. More and more cattle came pounding past the rampart of his victims, but always, it seemed, some elected to climb the heap of their dead and dying fellows, and Calhoun shot and shot...

But he split the herd. The foremost animals had been charging a sighted human enemy. Others had followed because it is the instinct of cattle to join their running fellows in whatever crazed urgency they feel. There was a dense, pounding, wailing, grunting, puffing, raising thick and impenetrable clouds of dust which hid everything but galloping beasts going past on either side.

It lasted for minutes. Then the thunder of hoofs diminished. It ended abruptly, and Calhoun and the girl were left alone with the gruesome pile of animals which had divided the charging herd into two parts. They could see the rears of innumerable running animals, stupidly continuing the charge, hardly different, now, from a stampede, whose original objective none now remembered.

Calhoun thoughtfully touched the barrel of his blast-rifle and winced at its scorching heat.

"I just realized," he said coldly, "that I don't know your name. What is it?"

"Maril," said the girl. She swallowed. "Th—thank you."

"Maril," said Calhoun, "you are an idiot! It was half-witted at best to go off by yourself! You could have been lost! You could have cost me days of hunting for you, days badly needed for more important matters!"

He stopped and took breath. "You may have spoiled what little chance I've got to do something about the plans Weald's already making! You have just acted with the most concentrated folly, and the most magnificent imbecility that you or anybody else could manage!"

He said more bitterly still, "And I had to leave Murgatroyd behind to get to you in time! He was right in the path of that charge!"

He turned away from her and said dourly, "All right! Come on back to the ship. We'll go to Dara. We'd have to, anyhow. But Murgatroyd—"

Then he heard a very small sneeze. Out of a rolling wall of still-roiling dust, Murgatroyd appeared forlornly. He was dust-covered, and draggled, and his tail dropped, and he sneezed again. He moved as if he could barely put one paw before another, but at sight of Calhoun he sneezed yet again and said "*Chee!*" in a disconsolate voice. Then he sat down and waited for Calhoun to come and pick him up.

When Calhoun did so, Murgatroyd clung to him pathetically and said "*Chee-chee!*" and again "*Chee-chee!*" with the intonation of one telling of incredible horrors and disasters endured. And as a matter of fact the escape of a small animal like Murgatroyd was remarkable. He'd escaped the trampling hoofs of at least hundreds of charging animals. Luck must have played a great part in it, but an hysterical agility in dodging must have been required, too.

Calhoun headed back for the valley where the settlement had been, and the Med Ship was. Murgatroyd clung to his neck. The girl Maril followed somewhat discouragedly. She was at that age when girls—and men of corresponding type—can grow most passionately devoted to ideals or causes in default of a promising personal romance. When concerned with such causes they can become splendidly confident that whatever they decide to do is sensible if only it is dramatic. But Maril was shaken, now.

Calhoun did not speak to her again. He led the way. A mile back toward the mountains, they began to see numerous stragglers from the now-vanished herd. A little farther on and those stragglers began to notice them. It would have been a matter of no moment if they'd been domesticated dairy cattle, but these were range cattle gone wild. Twice, Calhoun had to employ the use his blast-rifle to discourage incipient charges by irritated bulls or in some cases even more irritated cows. Those cows with calves were especially suspicious of Calhoun and his possible designs upon their offspring.

It was a relief to enter the valley again. But it was two miles more to the landing-grid with the Med Ship beside it and the reek of carrion in the air.

They were perhaps two hundred feet or more from the ship when the sound of a blast-rifle crashed and its bolt whined past Calhoun so close that he felt the monstrous heat. There had been no challenge. There was no warning. There was simply a shot which came horribly close to ending Calhoun's career in a completely arbitrary fashion.

CHAPTER FOUR

Five minutes later Calhoun had located one would-be killer behind a mass of splintered planking that once had been a wall. He set the wood afire by a blaster-bolt and then viciously sent other bolts all around the man it had sheltered when he fled from the flames. He could have killed him ten times over, but it was more desirable to open communication. So he missed intentionally.

Maril had cried out that she came from Dara and had word for them, but they did not answer. There were three men with heavy-duty blast-rifles. One was the one Calhoun had burned out of his hiding place. That man's rifle exploded when the flames hit it. Two remained.

One, so Calhoun presently discovered—was working his way behind underbrush to a shelf from which he could shoot down at Calhoun. Calhoun had dropped into a hollow and pulled Maril to cover at the first shot. The second man happily planned to get to a point where he could shoot him like a fish in a barrel.

The third man had fired half a dozen times and then disappeared. Calhoun estimated that he intended to get around to the rear, hoping there was no protection from that direction for Calhoun. It would take some time for him to manage it.

So Calhoun industriously concentrated his fire on the man trying to get above him. He was behind a boulder, not too dissimilar to Calhoun's breastwork. Calhoun set fire to the brush at the point at which the other man aimed. That, then, made his effort useless.

Then Calhoun sent a dozen bolts at the other man's rocky shield. It heated up. Steam rose in a whitish mass and blew directly away from Calhoun. He saw that antagonist flee. He saw him so clearly that he was positive that there was a patch of blue pigment on the right-hand side of the back of his neck.

He grunted and swung to find the third. That man moved through thick undergrowth, and Calhoun set it on fire in a neat pattern of spreading flames. Evidently, these men had had no training in battle tactics with blast-rifles. The third man also had to get away. He did. But something from him arched through the smoke. It fell to the ground directly upwind from Calhoun. White smoke puffed up violently.

It was instinct that made Calhoun react as he did. He jerked the girl Maril to her feet and rushed her toward the Med Ship. Smoke from the flung bomb upwind barely swirled around him and missed Maril altogether. Calhoun, though, got a whiff of something strange, not scorched or burning vegetation at all. He ceased to breathe and plunged onward. In clear air he emptied his lungs and refilled them. They were then halfway to the ship, with Murgatroyd prancing on ahead.

But then Calhoun's heart began to pound furiously. His muscles twitched and tensed. He felt extraordinary symptoms like an extreme of agitation. He swore, but a Med Ship man would not react to such symptoms as a non-medically-trained man would have done. Calhoun was familiar enough with tear gas, used by police on some planets.

But this was different and worse. Even as he helped and urged Maril onward, he automatically considered his sensations, and had it—panic gas. Police did not use it because panic is worse than rioting. Calhoun felt all the physical symptoms of fear and of gibbering terror.

A man whose mind yields to terror experiences certain physical sensations: wildly beating heart, tensed and twitching muscles, and a frantic impulse to convulsive action. A man in whom those physical sensations are induced by other means will, ordinarily, find his mind yielding to terror.

Calhoun couldn't combat his feelings, but his clinical attitude enabled him to act despite them. The three from Weald reached the base of the Med Ship. One of their enemies had lost his rifle and need not be counted. Another had fled from flames and might be ignored for some moments, anyhow. But a blast-bolt struck the ship's metal hull only feet from Calhoun, and he whipped around to the other side and let loose a staccato rat-tat-tat of fire which emptied the rifle of all its charges.

Then he opened the airlock door, hating the fact that he shook and trembled. He urged the girl and Murgatroyd in. He slammed the outer airlock door just as another blast-bolt hit.

"They—they don't realize," said Maril desperately. "If they only knew…"

"Talk to them, if you like," said Calhoun. His teeth chattered and he raged, because the symptom was of terror he denied.

He pushed a button on the control board. He pointed to a microphone. He got at an oxygen bottle and inhaled deeply. Oxygen, obviously, should be an antidote for panic, since the symptoms of terror act to increase the oxygenation of the bloodstream and muscles, and to make superhuman exertion possible if necessary.

Breathing ninety-five percent oxygen produced the effect the terror-inspiring gas strove for, so his heart slowed nearly to normal and his body relaxed. He held out his hand and it did not tremble. He'd been affronted to see it shake uncontrollably when he pushed the microphone button for Maril.

He turned to her. She hadn't spoken into the mike.

"They may not be from Dara!" she said shakily. "I just thought! They could be somebody else, maybe criminals who planned to raid the mine for a shipload of its ore."

"Nonsense," said Calhoun. "I saw one of them clearly enough to be sure. But they're skeptical characters. I'm afraid there may be more on the way here from wherever they keep themselves. Anyhow, now we know some of them are in hearing! I'll take advantage of that and we'll go on."

He took the microphone. An instant later his voice boomed in the stillness outside the ship, cutting through the thin shrill whirring of invisible small creatures.

"This is the Med Ship *Aesclipus Twenty*," said Calhoun's voice, amplified to a shout. "I left Weald four days ago, one day after the cargo ship from here arrived with everybody on board dead. On Weald they don't know how it happened, but they suspect blueskins. Sooner or later they'll search here.

"Get away! Cover up your tracks! Hide all signs that you've ever been here! Get the hell away, fast! One more warning! There's talk of fusion-bombing Dara. They're scared! If they find your traces, they'll be still more scared! So cover up your tracks and get away from here!"

The many-times-multiplied voice rolled and echoed among the hills. But it was very clear. Where it could be heard it could be understood, and it could be heard for miles.

But there was no response to it. Calhoun waited a reasonable time. Then he shrugged and seated himself at the control board.

"It isn't easy," he observed, "to persuade desperate men that they've outsmarted themselves! Hold hard, Murgatroyd!"

The rockets bellowed. Then there was a tremendous noise to end all noises, and the ship began to climb. It sped up and up and up. By the time it was out of atmosphere it had velocity enough to coast to clear space and Calhoun cut the rockets altogether.

He busied himself with those astrogational chores which began with orienting oneself to galactic directions after leaving a planet which rotates at its own individual speed. Then one computes the overdrive course to another planet, from the respecting coordinates of the world one is leaving and the one one aims for.

Then, in this case at any rate, there was the very finicky task of picking out a fourth-magnitude star of whose planets one was his destination. He aimed for it with ultra-fine precision.

"Overdrive coming," he said presently. "Hold on!"

Space reeled. There was nausea and giddiness and a horrible sensation of falling in a wildly unlikely spiral. Then stillness, and solidity, and the blackness outside the Med Ship. The little craft was in overdrive again.

After a long while, the girl Maril said uneasily, "I don't know what you plan now—"

"I'm going to Dara," said Calhoun. "On Orede I tried to get the blueskins there to get going, fast. Maybe I succeeded. I don't know. But this thing's been mishandled! Even if there's a famine people shouldn't do things out of desperation! Being desperate jogs the brain off-center. One doesn't think straight!"

"I know now that I was...very foolish."

"Forget it," commanded Calhoun. "I wasn't talking about you. Here I run into a situation that the Med Service should have caught and cleaned up generations ago! But it's not only a Med Service obligation; it's a current mess! Before I could begin to get at the basic problem, those idiots on Orede—It'd happened before I reached Weald! An emotional explosion triggered by a ship full of dead men that nobody intended to kill."

Maril shook her head.

"Those Darian characters," said Calhoun, annoyed, "shouldn't have gone to Orede in the first place. If they went there, they should at least have stayed on a continent where there were no people from Weald digging a mine and hunting cattle for sport on their off days! They could be spotted! I believe they were.

"And again, if it had been a long way from the mine installation, they could probably have wiped out the people who sighted them before they could get back with the news! But it looks like miners saw men hunting, and got close enough to see they were blueskins, and then got back to the mine with the news!"

She waited for him to explain.

"I know I'm guessing, but it fits!" he said distastefully. "So something had to be done. Either the mining settlement had to be wiped out or the story that blueskins were on Orede had to be discredited. The blueskins tried for both. They used panic gas on a herd of cattle and it made them crazy and they charged the settlement like the four-footed lunatics they are!

"And the blueskins used panic gas on the settlement itself as the cattle went through. It should have settled the whole business nicely. After it was over every man in the settlement would believe he'd been out of his head for a while, and he'd have the crazy state of the settlement to think about.

"He wouldn't be sure of what he'd seen or heard before-hand. They might try to verify the blueskin story later, but they wouldn't believe anything with certainty. It should have worked!"

Again she waited.

"Unfortunately, when the miners panicked, they stampeded into the ship. Also unfortunately, panic gas got into the ship with them. So they stayed panicked while the astrogator—in panic!—took off. They headed for Weald and threw on the overdrive—which would be set for Weald anyhow—because that would be the fastest way to run away from whatever he imagined he feared. But he and all the men on the ship were still crazy with panic from the gas they kept breathing until they died!"

Silence. After a long interval, Maril asked, "You don't think the Darians intended to kill?"

"I think they were stupid!" said Calhoun angrily. "Somebody's always urging the police to use panic gas in case of public tumult. But it's too dangerous. Nobody knows what one man will do in a panic. Take a hundred or two or three and panic them all, and there's no limit to their craziness! The whole thing was handled wrong!"

"But you don't blame them?"

"For being stupid, yes," said Calhoun fretfully. "But if I'd been in their place, perhaps—"

"Where were you born?" asked Maril suddenly.

Calhoun jerked his head around. "No! Not where you're guessing, or hoping. Not on Dara. Just because I act as if Darians were human doesn't mean I have to be one! I'm a Med Service man, and I'm acting as I think I should." His tone became exasperated.

"Dammit, I'm supposed to deal with health situations, actual, and possible causes of human deaths! And if Weald thinks it finds proof that blueskins are in space again and caused the death of Wealdians, it won't be healthy! They're halfway set anyhow to drop fusion-bombs on Dara to wipe it out!"

Maril said fiercely, "They might as well drop bombs. It'll be quicker than starvation, at least!"

Calhoun looked at her, more exasperated than before.

"It is a crop failure again?" he demanded. When she nodded he said bitterly, "Famine conditions already?" When she nodded again he said drearily, "And of course famine is the great-grandfather of health problems! And that's right in my lap with all the rest!"

He stood up. Then he sat down again.

"I'm tired!" he said flatly. "I'd like to get some sleep. Would you mind taking a book or something and going into the other cabin? Murgatroyd and I would like a little relaxation from reality. With luck, if I go to sleep, I may only have a nightmare. It'll be a terrific improvement on what I'm in now!"

Alone in the control compartment, he tried to relax, but it was not possible. He flung himself into a comfortable chair and brooded. There is brooding and brooding. It can be a form of wallowing in self-pity, engaged in for emotional satisfaction. But it can be, also, a way of bringing out unfavorable factors in a situation. A man in optimistic mood can ignore them. But no awkward situation is likely to be remedied while any of its elements are neglected.

Calhoun dourly considered the situation of the people of the planet Dara, which it was his job as a Med Service man to remedy or at least improve. Those people were marked by patches of blue pigment as an inherited consequence of a plague of three generations past. Because of the marking, which it was easy to believe a sign of continuing infection, they were hated and dreaded by their neighbors. Dara was a planet of pariahs—excluded from the human race by those who feared them.

And now there was famine on Dara for the second time, and they were of no mind to starve quietly. There was food on the planet Orede, monstrous herds of cattle without owners. It was natural enough for Darians to build a ship or ships and try to bring food back to its starving people. But that desperately necessary enterprise had now roused Weald to a frenzy of apprehension.

Weald was, if possible, more hysterically afraid of blueskins than ever before, and even more implacably the enemy of the starving planet's population. Weald itself prospered. Ironically, it had such an excess of foodstuffs that it stored them in unneeded spaceships in orbits about itself.

Hundreds of thousands of tons of grain circled Weald in sealed-tight hulks, while the people of Dara starved and only dared try to steal—if it could be called stealing—some of the innumerable wild cattle of Orede.

The blueskins on Orede could not trust Calhoun, so they pretended not to hear. Or maybe that didn't hear. They'd been abandoned and betrayed by all of humanity off their world. They'd been threatened and oppressed by guardships in orbit about them, ready to shoot down any spacecraft they might send aloft...

So Calhoun brooded, while Murgatroyd presently yawned and climbed to his cubbyhole and curled up to sleep with his furry tail carefully adjusted over his nose.

A long time later Calhoun heard small sounds which were not normal on a Med Ship in overdrive. They were not part of the random noises carefully generated to keep the silence of the ship endurable. Calhoun raised his head. He listened sharply. No sound could come from outside.

He knocked on the door of the sleeping cabin. The noises stopped instantly.

"Come out," he commanded through the door.

"I'm—I'm all right," said Maril's voice. But it was not quite steady. She paused. "Did I make a noise? I was having a bad dream."

"I wish," said Calhoun, "that you'd tell me the truth just occasionally! Come out, please!"

There were stirrings. After a little it opened and Maril appeared. She looked as if she'd been crying. She said, quickly, "I probably look queer, but it's because I was asleep."

"To the contrary," said Calhoun, fuming. "You've been lying awake crying. I don't know why. I've been out here wishing I could, because I'm frustrated. But since you aren't asleep maybe you can help me with my job. I've figured some things out. For some others I need facts. Will you give them to me?"

She swallowed. "I'll try."

"Coffee?" he asked.

Murgatroyd popped his head out of his miniature sleeping cabin.

"*Chee?*" he asked interestedly.

"Go back to sleep!" snapped Calhoun.

He began to pace back and forth.

"I need to know something about the pigment patches," he said jerkily. "Maybe it sounds crazy to think of such things now—first things first, you know. But this is a first thing! So long as Darians don't look like the people of other worlds, they'll be believed to be different. If they look repulsive, they'll be believed to be evil.

"Tell me about those patches. They're different sizes and different shapes and they appear in different places. You've none on your face or hands, anyhow."

"I haven't any at all," said the girl reservedly.

"I thought—"

"Not everybody," she said defensively. "Nearly, yes. But not all. Some people don't have them. Some people are born with bluish splotches on their skin, but they fade out while they're children. When they grow up they're just like the people of Weald or any other world. And their children never have them."

Calhoun stared.

"You couldn't possibly be proved to be a Darian, then?"

She shook her head. Calhoun remembered, and started the coffee.

"When you left Dara," he said, "you were carried a long, long way, to some planet where they'd practically never heard of Dara, and where the name meant nothing. You could have settled there, or anywhere else and forgotten about Dara. But you didn't. Why not, since you're not a blueskin?"

"But I am!" she said fiercely. "My parents, my brothers and sisters, and Korvan—"

Then she bit her lip. Calhoun took note but did not comment on the name she'd mentioned.

"Then your parents had the splotches fade, so you never had them," he said absorbedly. "Something like that happened on Tralee, once! There's a virus, a whole group of virus particles! Normally we humans are immune to them. One has to be in terrifically bad physical condition for them to take hold and produce whatever effects they do. But once they're established they're passed on from mother to child. And when they die out it's during childhood, too!"

He poured coffee for the two of them. Murgatroyd swung down to the floor and said, impatiently, "*Chee! Chee! Chee!*"

Calhoun absently filled Murgatroyd's tiny cup and handed it to him.

"But this is marvellous!" he said exuberantly. "The blue patches appeared after the plague, didn't they? After people recovered—when they recovered?"

Maril stared at him. His mind was filled with strictly professional considerations. He was not talking to her as a person. She was purely a source of information.

"So I'm told," said Maril reservedly. "Are there any more humiliating questions you want to ask?"

He gaped at her. Then he said ruefully, "I'm stupid, Maril, but you're touchy. There's nothing personal—"

"There is to me!" she said fiercely. "I was born among blueskins, and they're of my blood, and they're hated and I'd have been killed on Weald if I'd been known as...what I am! And there's Korvan, who arranged for me to be sent away as a spy and advised me to do just what you said: abandon my home world and everybody I care about! Including him! It's personal to me!"

Calhoun wrinkled his forehead helplessly.

"I'm sorry," he repeated. "Drink your coffee!"

"I don't want it," she said bitterly. "I'd like to die!"

"If you stay around where I am," Calhoun told her, "you may get your wish. All right, there'll be no more questions."

She turned and moved toward the door to the cabin. Calhoun looked after her.

"Maril."

"What?"

"Why were you crying?"

"You wouldn't understand," she said evenly.

Calhoun shrugged his shoulders almost up to his ears. He was a professional man. In his profession he was not incompetent. But there is no profession in which a really competent man tries to understand women. Calhoun, annoyed, had to let fate or chance or disaster take care of Maril's personal problems. He had larger matters to cope with.

But he had something to work on, now. He hunted busily in the reference tapes. He came up with an explicit collection of information on exactly the subject he needed. He left the control room to go down into the storage areas of the Med Ship's hull. He found an ultra frigid storage box, whose contents were kept at the temperature of liquid air.

He donned thick gloves, used a special set of tongs, and extracted a tiny block of plastic in which a sealed-tight phial of glass was embedded. It frosted instantly he took it out, and when the storage box was closed again the block was covered with a thick and opaque coating of frozen moisture.

He went back to the control room and pulled down the panel which made available a small-scale but surprisingly adequate biological laboratory. He set the plastic block in a container which would raise it very, very gradually to a specific temperature and hold it there. It was, obviously, a living culture from which any imaginable quantity of the same culture could be bred. Calhoun set the apparatus with great exactitude.

"This," he told Murgatroyd, "may be a good day's work. Now I think I can rest."

Then, for a long while, there was no sound or movement in the Med Ship. The girl may have slept, or maybe not. Calhoun lay relaxed in a chair which at the touch of a button became the most comfortable of sleeping places. Murgatroyd remained in his cubbyhole, his tail curled over his nose.

There were comforting, unheard, easily dismissable murmurings now and again. They kept the feeling of life alive in the ship. But for such infinitesimal stirrings of sound, carefully recorded for this exact purpose, the feel of the ship would have been that of a tomb.

But it was quite otherwise when another ship-day began with the taped sounds of morning activities as faint as echoes but nevertheless establishing an atmosphere of their own.

Calhoun examined the plastic block and its contents. He read the instruments which had cared for it while he slept. He put the block—no longer frosted—in the culture microscope and saw its enclosed, infinitesimal particles of life in the process of multiplying on the food that had been frozen with them when they were reduced to the spore condition. He beamed. He replaced the block in the incubation oven and faced the day cheerfully.

Maril greeted him with great reserve. They breakfasted, with Murgatroyd eating from his own platter on the floor, a tiny cup of coffee alongside.

"I've been thinking," said Maril evenly. "I think I can get you a hearing for whatever ideas you may have to help Dara."

"Kind of you," murmured Calhoun.

In theory, a Med Service man had all the authority needed for this or any other emergency. The power to declare a planet in quarantine, so cutting it off from all interstellar commerce, should be enough to force cooperation from any world's government. But in practice Calhoun had exactly as much power as he could exercise.

And Weald could not think straight where blueskins were concerned, and certainly the authorities on Dara could not be expected to be levelheaded. They had a history of isolation and outlawry, and long experience of being regarded as less than human. In cold fact, Calhoun had no power at all.

"May I ask whose influence you'll exert?" asked Calhoun.

"There's a man," said Maril reservedly, "who thinks a great deal of me. I don't know his present official position, but he was certain to become prominent. I'll tell him how you've acted up to now, and your attitude, and of course that you're Med Service. He'll be glad to help you, I'm sure."

"Splendid!" said Calhoun, nodding. "That will be Korvan."

She started. "How did you know?"

"Intuition," said Calhoun dryly. "All right. I'll count on him."

But he did not. He worked in the tiny biological lab all that ship-day and all the next. The girl was very quiet. Murgatroyd tried to enter into pretended conversation with her, but she was not able to match his pretense.

On the ship-day after, the time for breakout approached. While the ship was practically a world all by itself, it was easy to look forward with confidence to the future. But when contact and, in a fashion, conflict with other and larger worlds loomed nearer, prospects seemed less bright. Calhoun had definite plans, now, but there were so many ways in which they could be frustrated.

Calhoun sat down at the control board and watched the clock.

"I've got things lined up," he told Maril, "if only they work out. If I can make somebody on Dara listen, which is unlikely, and follow my advice, which they probably won't; and if Weald doesn't get the ideas it probably will get; and isn't doing what I suspect it is—why, maybe something can be done."

"I'm sure you'll do your best," said Maril politely.

Calhoun managed to grin. He watched the clock. There was no sensation attached to overdrive travel except at the beginning and the end. It was now time for the end. He might find most anything having happened. His plans might immediately be seen to be hopeless. Weald could have sent ships to Dara, or Dara might be in such a state of desperation...

As it turned out, Dara was desperate. The Med Ship came out nearly a light-month from the sun about which the planet Dara revolved. Calhoun went into a short hop toward it. Then Dara was on the other side of the blazing yellow star. It took time to reach it.

He called down, identifying himself and the ship and asking for coordinates so his ship could be brought to ground. There was confusion, as if the request were so unusual that the answers were not ready. The grid, too, was on the planet's night side. Presently the ship was locked onto by the grid's force-fields. It went downward.

Calhoun saw that Maril sat tensely, twisting her fingers within each other, until the ship actually touched ground.

Then he opened the exit port—and faced armed men in the darkness, with blast-rifles trained on him. There was a portable cannon trained on the Med Ship itself.

"Come out!" rasped a voice. "If you try anything you get blasted! Your ship and its contents are seized by the planetary government!"

CHAPTER FIVE

It seemed that the smell of hunger was in the air. The armed men were emaciated. Lights came on, and stark, harsh shadows lay black upon the ground. Calhoun's captors were uniformed, but the uniforms hung loosely upon them. Where the lights struck upon their faces, their cheeks were hollow. They were cadaverous. And there were the splotches of pigment of which Calhoun had heard.

The man nearest the Med Ship's port had a monstrous, irregular dull-blue marking over half of one side of his face and up upon his forehead. The man next to him had a blue throat. The next man again was less marked, but his left ear was blue and there was what seemed a splashing of the same color on the skin under his hair.

The leader of the truculent group—it might have been a firing squad—made an imperious gesture with his hand. It was blue, except for two fingers which in the glaring illumination seemed whiter than white.

"Out!" said that man savagely. "We're taking over your stock of food. You'll get your share of it, like everybody else, but—"

Maril spoke over Calhoun's shoulder. She uttered a cryptic sentence or two. It should have amounted to identification but there was skepticism in the armed party.

"Oh, you're one of us, eh?" said the guard leader sardonically. "You'll have a chance to prove that. Come out of there!"

Calhoun spoke abruptly, "This is a Med Ship," he said. "There are medicines and bacterial culture inside it. They shouldn't be meddled with. Here on Dara you've had enough of plagues!"

The man with the blue hand said as sardonically as before, "I said the government was taking over your ship! It won't be looted. But you're not taking a full cargo of food away! In fact, it's not likely you're leaving!"

"And I want to speak to someone in authority," snapped Calhoun. "We've just come from Weald." He felt bristling hatred all about him as he named Weald. "There's tumult there. They're talking about dropping fusion-bombs here. It's important that I talk to somebody with the authority to take a few sensible precautions!"

He descended to the ground. There was a panicky "*Chee! Chee!*" from behind him, and Murgatroyd came dashing to swarm up his body and cling apprehensively to his neck.

"What's that?"

"A *tormal*," said Calhoun. "He's not a pet. Your medical men will know something about him. This is a Med Ship and I'm a Med Ship man, and he's an important member of the crew. He's a Med Ship *tormal* and he stays with me!"

The man with the blue hand said harshly, "There's somebody waiting to ask you questions. Here!"

A groundcar came rolling out from the side of the landing-grid enclosure. The groundcar ran on wheels, and wheels were not much used on modern worlds. Dara was behind the times in more ways than one.

"This car will take you to Defense and you can tell them anything you want. But don't try to sneak back in this ship! It'll be guarded!"

The groundcar was enclosed, with room for a driver and the three from the Med Ship. But armed men festooned themselves about its exterior and it went bumping and rolling to the massive ground-layer girders of the grid. It rolled out under them and onto a paved highway. It picked up speed.

There were buildings on either side of the road, but few showed lights. This was night, and the men at the landing-grid had set a pattern of hunger, so that the silence and the dark buildings did not seem a sign of tranquility and sleep, but of exhaustion and despair.

The highway lamps were few, by comparison with other inhabited worlds, and the groundcar needed lights of its own to guide its driver over a paved surface that needed repair. By those moving lights other depressing things could be seen: untidiness, buildings not kept up to perfection, evidences of apathy, the road, which hadn't been cleaned lately, litter here and there.

Even the fact that there were no stars added to the feeling of wretchedness and gloom and, ultimately, of hunger.

Maril spoke nervously to the driver.

"The famine isn't any better?"

He moved his head in negation, but did not speak. There was a splotch of blue pigment at the back of his neck. It extended upward into his hair.

"I left two years ago," said Maril. "It was just beginning then. Rationing hadn't started."

The driver said evenly, "There's rationing now!"

The car went on and on. A vast open space appeared ahead. Lights about its perimeter seemed few and pale.

"Everything seems worse. Even the lights."

"Using all the power," said the driver, "to warm up ground to grow crops where it ought to be winter. Not doing too well, either."

Calhoun knew, somehow, that Maril moistened her lips.

"I was sent," she explained to the driver, "to go ashore on Trent and then make my way to Weald. I mailed reports of what I found out back to Trent. Somebody got them back to here whenever it was possible."

The driver said, "Everybody knows the man on Trent disappeared. Maybe he got caught, maybe somebody saw him without make-up. Or maybe he just quit being one of us. What's the difference? No use!"

Calhoun found himself wincing a little. The driver was not angry. He was hopeless. But men should not despair. They shouldn't accept hostility from those about them as a device of fate for their destruction.

Maril said quickly to Calhoun, "You understand? Dara's a heavy-metals planet. There aren't many light elements in our soil. Potassium is scarce. So our ground isn't very fertile. Before the Plague we traded metals and manufactured products for imports of food and potash. But since the Plague we've had no off-planet commerce. We've been quarantined."

"I gathered as much," said Calhoun. "It was up to Med Service to see that that didn't happen. It's up to Med Service now to see that it stops."

"Too late now for anything," said the driver. "Whatever Med Service may be! They're talking about cutting down our population so there'll be food enough for some to live. There are two questions about it. One is who's to be kept alive, and the other is why."

The groundcar aimed now for a cluster of faintly brighter lights on the far side of the great open space.

They enlarged as they grew nearer. Maril said hesitantly, "There was someone, Korvan—" Calhoun didn't catch the rest of the name. Maril said hesitantly, "He was working on food plants. I thought he might accomplish something…"

The driver said caustically, "Sure! Everybody's heard about him! He came up with a wonderful thing! He and his outfit worked out a way to process weeds so they can be eaten. And they can. You can fill your belly and not feel hungry, but it's like eating hay. You starve just the same. He's still working. Head of a government division."

The groundcar passed through a gate. It stopped before a lighted door. The armed men hanging to its outside dropped off. They watched Calhoun closely as he stepped out with Murgatroyd riding on his shoulder.

Minutes later they faced a hastily summoned group of officials of the Darian government. For a ship to land on Dara was so remarkable an event that it called practically for a cabinet meeting. And Calhoun noted that they were no better fed than the guards at the spaceport.

They regarded Calhoun and Maril with oddly burning, eyes. It was, of course, because the two of them showed no signs of hunger. They obviously had not been on short rations. Darians had this, now, to increase a hatred which was inevitable anyhow, directed at all peoples off their own planet.

"My name is Calhoun," said Calhoun briskly. "I've the usual Med Service credentials. Now—"

He did not wait to be questioned. He told them of the appalling state of things in the Twelfth Sector of the Med Service, so that men had been borrowed from other sectors to remedy the intolerable, and he was one of them. He told of his arrival at Weald and what had happened there, from the excessively cautious insistence that he prove he was not a Darian, to the arrival of the death-ship from Orede.

He was giving them the news affecting them, as they had not heard it before. He went on to tell of his stop at Orede and his purpose, and his encounter with the men he found there. When he finished there was silence. He broke it.

"Now," he said, "Maril's an agent of yours. She can add to what I've told you. I'm Med Service. I have a job to do here to carry out what wasn't done before. I should make a planetary health inspection and make recommendations for the improvement of the state of things. I'll be glad if you'll arrange for me to talk to your health officials. Things look bad, and something should be done."

Someone laughed without mirth.

"What will you recommend for long-continued undernourishment?" he asked derisively. "That's our health problem!"

"I recommend food," said Calhoun.

"Where'll you fill the prescription?"

"I've the answer to that, too," said Calhoun curtly. "I'll want to talk to any space pilots you've got. Get your astrogators together and I think they'll approve my idea."

The silence was totally skeptical.

"Orede—"

"Not Orede," said Calhoun. "Weald will be hunting that planet over for Darians. If they find any, they'll drop bombs here."

"Our only space pilots," said a tall man, presently, "are on Orede now. If you've told the truth, they'll probably head back because of your warning. They should bring meat."

His mouth worked peculiarly, and Calhoun knew that it was at the thought of food.

"Which," said another man sharply, "goes to the hospitals! I haven't tasted meat in two years!"

"Nobody has," growled another man still. "But here's this man Calhoun. I'm not convinced he can work magic, but we can find out if he lies. Put a guard on his ship. Otherwise let our health men give him his head. They'll find out if he's from this Medical Service he tells of! and this Maril…"

"I can be identified," said Maril. "I was sent to gather information and send it in secret writing to one of us on Trent. I have a family here. They'll know me! And I—there was someone who was working on foods, and I believe he made it possible to use…all sorts of vegetation for food. He will identify me."

Someone laughed harshly.

Maril swallowed.

"I'd like to see him," she repeated. "And my family."

Some of the blue-splotched men turned away. A broad-shouldered man said bluntly, "Don't look for them to be glad to see you. And you'd better not show yourself in public. You've been well fed. You'll be hated for that."

Maril began to cry. Murgatroyd said bewilderedly, *"Chee! Chee!"*

Calhoun held him close. There was confusion. And Calhoun found the Minister of Health at hand. He looked most harried of all the officials gathered to question Calhoun. He proposed that he get a look at the hospital situation right away.

It wasn't practical. With all the population on half rations or less, when night came people needed to sleep. Most people, indeed, slept as many hours out of the

THIS WORLD IS TABOO

traditional twenty-four as they could manage. It was much more pleasant to sleep than to be awake and constantly nagged at by continued hunger.

And there was the matter of simple decency. Continuous gnawing hunger had an embittering effect upon everyone. Quarrelsomeness was a common experience. And people who would normally be the leaders of opinion felt shame because they were obsessed by thoughts of food. It was best when people slept.

Still, Calhoun was in the hospitals by daybreak. What he found moved him to savage anger. There were too many sick children. In every case undernourishment contributed to their sickness. And there was not enough food to make them well. Doctors and nurses denied themselves food to spare it for their patients. And most of that self-denial was doubtless voluntary, but it would not be discreet for anybody on Dara to look conspicuously better fed than his fellows.

Calhoun brought out hormones and enzymes and medicaments from the Med Ship while the guard in the ship looked on. He demonstrated the processes of synthesis and auto-catalysis that enabled such small samples to be multiplied indefinitely. He was annoyed by a clamorous appetite. There were some doctors who ignored the irony of medical techniques being taught to cure nonnutritional disease, when everybody was half-fed, or less. They approved of Calhoun. They even approved of Murgatroyd when Calhoun explained his function.

He was, of course, a Med Service *tormal*, and *tormals* were creatures of talent. They'd originally been found on a planet in the Deneb area, and they were engaging and friendly small animals. But the remarkable fact about them was that they couldn't contract any disease. Not any.

They had a built-in, explosive reaction to bacterial and viral toxins, and there hadn't yet been any pathogenic organism discovered to which a *tormal* could not more or less immediately develop antibody resistance. So that in interstellar medicine *tormals* were priceless.

Let Murgatroyd be infected with however localized, however specialized an inimical organism, and presently some highly valuable defensive substance could be isolated from his blood and he'd remain in his usual exuberant good health.

When the antibody was analyzed by those techniques of microanalysis the Service had developed, that was that. The antibody could be synthesized and one could attack any epidemic with confidence.

The tragedy for Dara was, of course, that no Med Ship had come to Dara three generations ago, when the Dara plague raged. Worse, after the plague Weald was able to exert pressure which only a criminally incompetent Med Service director would have permitted. But criminal incompetence and its consequences was what Calhoun had been loaned to Sector Twelve to help remedy. He was not at ease, though. No ship arrived from Orede to bear out his account of an attempt to get that lonely world evacuated before Weald discovered it had blueskins on it. Maril had vanished, to visit or return to her family, or perhaps to consult with the mysterious Korvan who'd arranged for her to leave Dara to be a spy, and had advised her simply to make a new life somewhere else, abandoning a famine-ridden, despised, and out-caste world.

Calhoun had learned of two achievements the same Korvan had made for his world. Neither was remarkably constructive. He'd offered to prove the value of the second by dying of it. Which might make him a very admirable character, or he could have a passion for martyrdom, which is much more common than most people think. In two days Calhoun was irritable enough from unaccustomed hunger to suspect the worst of him.

Meanwhile Calhoun worked doggedly; in the hospitals while the patients were awake and in the Med Ship, under guard, afterward. He had hunger cramps now, but he tested a plastic cube with a thriving biological culture in it.

He worked at increasing his store of it. He'd snipped samples of pigmented skin from dead patients in the hospitals, and examined the pigmented areas, and very, very painstakingly verified a theory. It took an electron microscope to do it, but he found a virus in the blue patches which matched the type discovered on Tralee.

The Tralee viruses had effects which were passed on from mother to child, and heredity had been charged with the observed results of quasi-living viral particles. And then Calhoun very, very carefully introduced into a virus culture the material he had been growing in a plastic cube. He watched what happened.

He was satisfied, so much so that immediately afterward he yawned and yawned and barely managed to stagger off to bed. The watching guard in the Med Ship watched him in amazement.

That night the ship from Orede came in, packed with frozen bloody carcasses of cattle. Calhoun knew nothing of it. But next morning Maril came back. There were shadows under her eyes and her expression was of someone who has lost everything that had meaning in her life.

"I'm all right," she insisted, when Calhoun commented. "I've been visiting my family. I've seen Korvan. I'm quite all right."

"You haven't eaten any better than I have," Calhoun observed.

"I couldn't!" admitted Maril. "My sisters, my little sisters so thin... There's rationing for everybody and it's all efficiently arranged. They even had rations for me. But I couldn't eat! I gave most of my food to my sisters and they—they squabbled over it!"

Calhoun said nothing. There was nothing to say. Then she said, in a no less desolate tone, "Korvan said I was foolish to come back."

"He could be right," said Calhoun.

"But I had to!" protested Maril. "And now I—I've been eating all I wanted to, in Weald and in the ship, and I'm ashamed because they're half-starved and I'm not. And when you see what hunger does to them... It's terrible to be half-starved and not able to think of anything but food!"

"I hope," said Calhoun, "to do something about that. If I can get hold of an astrogator or two—"

"The ship that was on Orede came in during the night," Maril told him shakily. "It was loaded with frozen meat, but one load's not enough to make a difference on a whole planet! And if Weald hunts for us on Orede, we daren't go back for more meat."

She said abruptly, "There are some prisoners. They were miners. They were crowded out of the ship. The Darians who'd stampeded the cattle took them prisoners. They had to!"

"True," said Calhoun. "It wouldn't have been wise to leave Wealdians around on Orede with their throats cut. Or living, either, to tell about a rumor of blueskins. Even if their throats will be cut now. Is that the program?"

Maril shivered.

"No. They'll be put on short rations like everybody else. And people will watch them. The Wealdians expect to die of plague any minute because they've been with Darians. So people look at them and laugh. But it's not very funny."

"It's natural," said Calhoun, "but perhaps lacking in charity. Look there! How about those astrogators? I need them for a job I have in mind."

Maril wrung her hands.

"C—come here," she said in a low tone.

There was an armed guard in the control room of the ship. He'd watched Calhoun a good part of the previous day as Calhoun performed his mysterious work. He'd been off-duty and now was on duty again. He was bored. So long as Calhoun did not touch the control board, though, he was uninterested. He didn't even turn his head when Maril led the way into the other cabin and slid the door shut.

"The astrogators are coming," she said swiftly. "They'll bring some boxes with them. They'll ask you to instruct them so they can handle our ship better. They lost themselves coming back from Orede. No, they didn't lose themselves, but they lost time, enough time almost to make an extra trip for meat. They need to be experts. I'm to come along, so they can be sure that what you teach them is what you've been doing right along."

Calhoun said, "Well?"

"They're crazy!" said Maril vehemently. "They knew Weald would do something monstrous sooner or later. But they're going to try to stop it by being more monstrous sooner! Not everybody agrees, but there are enough. So they want to use your ship—it's faster in overdrive and so on. And they'll go to Weald in this ship and—they say they'll give Weald something to keep it busy without bothering us!"

Calhoun said dryly, "This pays me off for being too sympathetic with blueskins! But if I'd been hungry for a couple of years, and was despised to boot by the people who kept me hungry, I suppose I might react the same way. No," he said curtly as she opened her lips to speak again, "don't tell me the trick. Considering everything, there's only one trick it could be. But I doubt profoundly that it would work. All right."

He slid the door back and returned to the control room. Maril followed him. He said detachedly, "I've been working on a problem outside of the food one. It isn't the time to talk about it right now, but I think I've solved it."

Maril turned her head, listening. There were footsteps on the tarmac outside the ship. Both doors of the airlock were open. Four men came in. They were young men who did not look quite as hungry as most Darians, but there was a reason for that. Their leader introduced himself and the others. They were the astrogators of the ship Dara had built to try to bring food from Orede. They were not, said their self-appointed leader, good enough. They'd overshot their destination. They came out of overdrive too far off line. They needed instruction.

Calhoun nodded, and observed that he'd been asking for them. They were, of course, blueskins. On one the only visible disfigurement was a patch of blue upon his wrist. On another the appearance of a blue birthmark appeared beside his eye and went back and up his temple. A third had a white patch on his temple, with all the rest of his face a dull blue. The fourth had blue fingers on one hand.

"We've got orders," said their leader, steadily, "to come on board and learn from you how to handle this ship. It's better than the one we've got."

"I asked for you," repeated Calhoun. "I've an idea I'll explain as we go along... Those boxes?"

Someone was passing in iron boxes through the airlock. One of the four very carefully brought them inside.

"They're rations," said a second young man. "We don't go anywhere without rations, except Orede."

"Orede, yes. I think we were shooting at each other there," said Calhoun pleasantly. "Weren't we?"

"Yes," said the young man.

He was neither cordial nor antagonistic. He was impassive. Calhoun shrugged.

"Then we can take off immediately. Here's the communicator and there's the button. You might call the grid and arrange for us to be lifted."

The young man seated himself at the control board. Very professionally, he went through the routine of preparing to lift by landing-grid, which routine has not changed in two hundred years. He went briskly ahead until the order to lift. Then Calhoun stopped him.

"Hold it!"

He pointed to the airlock. Both doors were open. The young man at the control board flushed vividly. One of the others closed and dogged the doors.

The ship lifted. Calhoun watched with seeming negligence. But he found occasion for a dozen corrections of procedure. This was presumably a training voyage of his own suggestion. Therefore, when the blueskin pilot would have flung the Med Ship into undirected overdrive, Calhoun grew stern. He insisted on a destination. He suggested Weald.

The young men glanced at each other and accepted the suggestion. He made the acting pilot look up the intrinsic brightness of its sun and measure its apparent brightness from just off Dara. He made him estimate the change in brightness to be expected after so many hours in overdrive, if one broke out to measure.

The first blueskin student pilot ended a Calhoun-determined tour of duty with more respect for Calhoun then he'd had at the beginning. The second was anxious to show up better than the first. Calhoun drilled him in the use of brightness-charts, by which the changes in apparent brightness of stars between overdrive hops could be correlated with angular changes to give a three-dimensional picture of the nearer heavens.

It was a highly necessary art which had not been worked out on Dara, and the prospective astrogators became absorbed in this and other fine points of space-piloting. They'd done enough, in a few trips to Orede, to realize that they needed to know more. Calhoun showed them.

Calhoun did not try to make things easy for them. He was hungry and easily annoyed. It was sound training tactics to be severe, and to phrase all suggestions as commands. He put the four young men in command of the ship in turn, under his direction. He continued to use Weald as a destination, but he set up problems in which the Med Ship came out of overdrive pointing in an unknown direction and with a precessory motion.

He made the third of his students identify Weald in the celestial globe containing hundreds of millions of stars, and get on course in overdrive toward it. The fourth suddenly required to compute the distance to Weald from such data as he could get from observation, without reference to any records.

By this time the first man was chafing to take a second turn. Calhoun gave each of them a second gruelling lesson. He gave them, in fact, a highly condensed but very sound course in the art of travel in space. His young students took command in four-hour watches, with at least one breakout from overdrive in each watch.

He built up enthusiasm in them. They ignored the discomfort of being hungry—though there had been no reason for them to stint on food on Orede—in growing pride in what they came to know.

When Weald was a first-magnitude star, the four were not highly qualified astrogators, to be sure, but they were vastly better spacemen than at the beginning. Inevitably, their attitude toward Calhoun was respectful. He'd been irritable and right. To the young, the combination is impressive.

Maril had served as passenger only. In theory she was to compare Calhoun's lessons with his practise when alone. But he did nothing on this journey which, teaching considered, was different from the two interstellar journeys Maril had made with him.

She occupied the sleeping cabin during two of the six watches of each ship-day. She operated the food-readier, which was almost completely emptied of its original store of food, it having been confiscated by the government of Dara. That amount of food would make no difference to the planet, but it was wise for everyone on Dara to be equally ill-fed.

On the sixth day out from Dara, the sun of Weald had a magnitude of minus five-tenths. The electron telescope could detect its larger planets, especially a gas-giant fifth-orbit world of high albedo. Calhoun had his four students estimate its distance again, pointing out the difference that could be made in breakout position if the Med Ship were mis-aimed by as much as one second of arc.

"And now," he said briskly, "we'll have coffee. I'm going to graduate you as pilots. Maril, four cups of coffee, please."

Murgatroyd said *"Chee?"* The Med Ship was badly crowded with six humans and Murgatroyd in a space intended for Calhoun and Murgatroyd alone. The little *tormal* had spent most of his time in his cubbyhole, watching with beady eyes as so many people moved about on what had been a spacious ship before.

"No coffee for you, Murgatroyd," said Calhoun. "You didn't do your lessons. This is for the graduating class only."

Murgatroyd came out of his miniature den. He found his little cup and offered it insistently, saying, *"Chee! Chee! Chee!"*

"No!" said Calhoun firmly. He regarded his class of four young men with their blueskin markings. "Drink it down!" he commanded. "That's the last order I'll give you. You're graduate pilots, now!"

They drank the coffee with a flourish. There was not one who did not admire Calhoun for having made them admire themselves. They were, actually, almost as much better pilots as they believed.

"And now," said Calhoun, "I suppose you'll tell me the truth about those boxes you brought on board. You said they were rations, but they haven't been opened in six days. I have an idea what they mean, but you tell me."

The four looked uncomfortable. There was a long pause.

"They could be," said Calhoun detachedly, "cultures to be dumped on Weald. Weald is making plans to wipe out

Dara. So some fool has decided to get Weald too busy fighting a plague of its own to bother with you. Is that right?"

The young men stirred unhappily. Young men can very easily be made into fanatics. But they have to be kept stirred up. They can't be provided with sound reason for self-respect. On the Med Ship there'd not been a single reference to Weald except as an object toward which the Med Ship was being astrogated. There'd been no reference to blueskins or enemies or threats or anything but space-piloting. The four young men were now fanatical about the proper handling of a ship in emptiness.

"Well, sir," said one of them, unhappily, "that's what we were ordered to do."

"I object," said Calhoun. "It wouldn't work. I just left Weald a little while back, remember. They've been telling themselves that some day Dara would try that. They've made preparations to fight any imaginable contagion you could drop on them. Every so often somebody claims it's happening. It wouldn't work. I object!"

"But—"

"In fact," said Calhoun, "I forbid it. I shall prevent it. You shan't do anything of the kind."

One of the young men, staring at Calhoun, nodded suddenly. His eyes closed. He jerked his head erect and looked bewildered. A second sank heavily into a chair. He said remotely, "Thish sfunny!" and abruptly went to sleep. The third found his knees giving way. He paid elaborate attention to them, stiffening them. But they yielded like rubber and he went slowly down to the floor. The fourth said thickly and reproachfully, "Thought y'were our frien'!"

He collapsed.

Calhoun very soberly tied them hand and foot and laid them out comfortably on the floor. Maril watched, white-faced, her hand to her throat. Murgatroyd looked agitated. He said anxiously, "*Chee? Chee?*"

"No," said Calhoun. "They'll wake up presently."

Maril said in a tense and desperate whisper, "You're betraying us! You're going to take us to Weald!"

"No," said Calhoun. "We'll only orbit around it. First, though, I want to get rid of those damned packed-up cultures. They're dead, by the way. I killed them with super-sonics a couple of days ago, while a fine argument was going on about distance-measurements by variable Cepheids of known period."

He put the four boxes carefully in the disposal unit. He operated it. The boxes and their contents streamed out to space in the form of metallic and other vapors. Calhoun sat at the control desk.

"I'm a Med Service man," he said detachedly. "I couldn't cooperate in the spread of plagues, anyhow, though a useful epidemic might be another matter. But the important thing right now is not keeping Weald busy with troubles to increase their hatred of Dara. It's getting some food for Dara. And driblets won't help. What's needed is thousands of tons, or tens of thousands." Then he said, "Overdrive coming, Murgatroyd! Hold fast!"

The universe vanished. The customary unpleasant sensations accompanied the change. Murgatroyd burped.

CHAPTER SIX

A large part of the firmament was blotted out by the blindingly bright half-disk of Weald, as it shone in the sunshine. It had icecaps at its poles, and there were seas, and the mottled look of land which had that carefully maintained balance of woodland and cultivated areas which was so effective in climate control. The Med Ship floated free, and Calhoun fretfully monitored all the beacon frequencies known to man.

There was relative silence inside the ship. Maril watched Calhoun in a sort of despairing indecision. The four young blueskins still slept, still bound hand and foot upon the control room floor. Murgatroyd regarded them, and Maril, and Calhoun in turn, and his small and furry forehead wrinkled helplessly.

"They can't have landed what I'm looking for!" protested Calhoun as his search had no result. "They can't! It would be too sensible for them to have done it!"

Murgatroyd said *"Chee!"* in a subdued voice.

"But where the devil did they put them?" demanded Calhoun. "A polar orbit would be ridiculous! They—" Then he grunted in disgust. "Oh! Of course! Now, where's the landing-grid?"

He worked busily for minutes, checking the position of the Wealdian landing-grid, which was mapped in the Sector Directory, against the look of continents and seas on the half-disk so plainly visible outside. He found what he wanted. He put on the ship's solar system drive.

"I wish," he complained to Maril, "I wish I could think straight the first time! And it's so obvious! If you want to put something out in space, and not have it interfere with traffic, in what sort of orbit and at what distance will you put it?"

Maril did not answer.

"Obviously," said Calhoun, "you'll put it as far as possible from the landing-pattern of ships coming in to the spaceport. You'll put it on the opposite side of the planet. And you'll want it to stay out of the way, where anybody can know it is at any time of the day or night without having to calculate anything.

"So you'll put it out in orbit so it will revolve around Weald in exactly one day, neither more nor less, and you'll put it above the equator. And then it will remain quite stationary above one spot on the planet, a hundred and eighty degrees longitude away from the landing-grid and directly over the equator."

He scribbled for a moment.

"Which means forty-two thousand miles high, give or take a few hundred, and—here! And I was hunting for it in a close-in orbit!"

He grumbled to himself. He waited while the solar-system drive pushed the Med Ship a quarter of the way around the bright planet below. The sunset line vanished and the planet's disk became a complete circle. Then Calhoun listened to the monitor earphones again, and grunted once more, and changed course, and presently made a noise indicating satisfaction.

He abandoned instrument control and peered directly out of a port, handling the solar system drive with great care. Murgatroyd said depressedly, "*Chee!*"

"Stop worrying," commanded Calhoun. "We haven't been challenged, and there is a beacon transmitter at work, just to make sure that nobody bumps into what we're looking for. It's a great help, because we do want to bump, but gently."

Stars swung across the port out of which he looked. Something dark appeared, and then straight lines and exact curvings. Even Maril, despairing and bewildered as she was, caught sight of something vastly larger than the Med Ship, floating in space. She stared. The Med Ship maneuvered very cautiously. She saw another large object. A third. A fourth. There seemed to be dozens of them.

They were spaceships, huge by comparison with *Aesclipus Twenty*. They floated as the Med Ship did. They did not drive. They were not in formation. They were not at even distances from each other. They did not point in the same direction. They swung in emptiness like derelicts.

Calhoun jockeyed his small ship with infinite care. Presently there came the gentlest of impacts and then a clanking sound. The appearance out the vision port became stationary, but still unbelievable. The Med Ship was grappled magnetically to a vast surface of welded metal.

Calhoun relaxed. He opened a wall panel and brought out a vacuum suit. He began briskly to get it on.

"Things moving smoothly," he commented. "We weren't challenged. So it's extremely unlikely that we were spotted. Our friends on the floor ought to begin to come to shortly. And I'm going to find out now whether I'm a hero or in sure-enough trouble!"

Maril said drearily, "I don't know what you've done, except—"

Calhoun blinked at her, in the act of hauling the vacuum suit up his chest and over his shoulders.

"Isn't it self-evident?" he demanded. "I've been giving astrogation lessons to these characters. I certainly didn't do it to help them dump germ-cultures on Weald! I brought them here! Don't you see the point? These are space ships. They're in orbit around Weald. They're not manned and they're not controlled. In fact, they're nothing but sky-riding storage bins!"

He seemed to consider the explanation complete. He wriggled his arms into the sleeves and gloves of the suit. He slung the air tanks over his shoulder and hooked them to the suit.

"I'll be back," he said. "I hope with good news. I've reason to be hopeful, though, because these Wealdians are very practical men. They have things all prepared and tidy. I suspect I'll find these ships with stores of air and fuel, maybe even food, so that if Weald should manage to make a deal for the stuff stored out here in them, they'd only have to bring out crews."

He lifted the space helmet down from its rack and put it on. He tested it, reading the tank air-pressure, power-storage, and other data from the lighted miniature instruments visible through pinholes above his eye-level. He fastened a space rope about himself, speaking through the helmet's opened faceplate.

"If our friends should wake up before I get back," he added, "please restrain them. I'd hate to be marooned."

He went waddling into the airlock with the coil of space rope over one vacuum-suited arm. The inner lock door closed behind him. A little later Maril heard the outer lock open. Then silence.

Murgatroyd whimpered a little. Maril shivered. Calhoun had gone out of the ship to nothingness. He'd said that what he was looking for, and what he'd found, was forty-two thousand miles from Weald. One could imagine falling forty-two thousand miles, where one couldn't imagine falling a light-year.

Calhoun was walking on the steel plates of a gigantic spaceship which floated among dozens of its fellows, all seeming derelicts and seemingly abandoned. He was able to walk on the nearest because of magnetic-soled shoes. He trusted his life to them and to a flimsy space rope which trailed after him out the Med Ship's airlock.

Time passed. A clock ticked in that hurried tempo of five ticks to the second which has been the habit of clocks since time immemorial. Very small and trivial noises came from the background tape, preventing utter silence from hanging intolerably in the ship.

Maril found herself listening tensely for something else. One of the four bound blueskins snored, and stirred, and slept again. Murgatroyd gazed about unhappily, and swung down to the control room floor, and then paused for lack of any place to go or anything to do. He sat down and began half-heartedly to lick his whiskers. Maril stirred.

Murgatroyd looked at her hopefully.

"*Chee?*" he asked shrilly.

She shook her head. It became a habit to act as if Murgatroyd were a human being. "No," she said unsteadily. "Not yet."

More time passed. An unbearably long time. Then there was the faintest of clankings. It repeated. Then, abruptly, there were noises in the airlock. They continued. They were fumbling noises.

The outer airlock door closed. The inner door opened. Dense white fog came out of it. There was motion. Calhoun followed the fog out of the lock. He carried objects which had been weightless, but were suddenly heavy in the ship's gravity-field. There were two spacesuits and a curious assortment of parcels. He spread them out, flipped aside his faceplate, and said briskly, "This stuff is cold! Turn a heater on it, will you, Maril?"

He began to work his way out of his own vacuum-suit.

"Item," he said. "The ships are fuelled *and* provisioned. A practical tribe, the Wealdians! The ships are ready to take off as soon as they're warmed up inside. A half-degree sun doesn't radiate heat enough to keep a ship warm, when the rest of the cosmos is effectively near zero Kelvin. Here, point the heaters like this."

He adjusted the radiant-heat dispensers. The fog disappeared where their beams played. But the metal spacesuits glistened and steamed, and the steam disappeared within inches. They were so completely and utterly cold that they condensed the air about them as a liquid, which re-evaporated to make fog, which warmed up and disappeared and was immediately replaced.

"Item," said Calhoun again, getting his arms out of the vacuum-suit sleeves. "The controls are pretty nearly standard. Our sleeping friends will be able to astrogate them back to Dara without trouble, provided only that nobody comes out here to bother us before they leave."

He shed the last of the spacesuit, stepping out of its legs.

"And," he finished wryly, "I brought back an emergency supply of ship provisions for everybody concerned, but find that I'm idiot enough to feel that they'll choke me if I eat them while Dara's still starving."

Maril said, "But there isn't any hope for Dara! No real hope!"

He gaped at her.

"What do you think we're here for?"

He set to work to restore his four recent students to consciousness. It was not a difficult task. The dosage mixed in the coffee given them as a graduation ceremony—the ceremony which had consisted solely of drinking coffee and passing out—allowed for waking-up processes. Calhoun took the precaution of disarming them first, but presently four hot-eyed young men glared at him.

"I'm calling," said Calhoun, holding a blaster negligently in his hand, "I'm calling for volunteers. There's a famine on Dara. There've been unmanageable crop surpluses on Weald. On Dara, the government grimly rations every ounce of food. On Weald, the government has been buying surplus grain to keep the price up.

"To save storage costs, it's loaded the grain into out-of-date spaceships it once used to stand sentry over Dara to keep it out of space when there was another famine there. Those ships have been put out in orbit, where we're hooked on to one of them.

"It's loaded with half a million bushels of grain. I've brought spacesuits from it, I've turned on the heaters in its interior, and I've set its overdrive unit for a hop to Dara. Now I'm calling for volunteers to take half a million bushels of grain to where it's needed. Do I get any volunteers?"

He got four. Not immediately, because they were ashamed that he'd made it impossible to carry out their original fanatic plan, and now offered something much better to make up for it. They raged. But half a million bushels of grain meant that people who must otherwise die might live.

Ultimately, truculently, first one and then another angrily agreed.

"Good!" said Calhoun. "Now, how many of you dare risk the trip alone? I've got one grain ship warming up. There are plenty of others around us. Every one of you can take a ship and half a million bushels to Dara, if you have the nerve!"

The atmosphere changed. Suddenly they clamored for the task he offered them. They were still acutely uncomfortable. He'd bossed them and taught them until they felt capable and glamorous and proud. Then he'd pinned their ears back. But if they returned to Dara with four enemy ships and unimaginable quantities of food with which to break the famine...

There was work to be done first, of course. Only one ship was so far warming up. Three more had to be entered, in spacesuits, and each had to have its interior warmed so breathable air could exist inside it, and at least part of the stored provisions had to be brought up to reasonable temperature for use on the journey.

Then the overdrive unit had to be inspected and set for the length of journey that a direct overdrive hop to Dara would mean, and Calhoun had to make sure again that each of the four could identify Dara's sun under all circumstances and aim for it with the requisite high precision, both before going into overdrive and after breakout. When all that was accomplished, Calhoun might reasonably hope that they'd arrive. But it wasn't a certainty.

Still, presently his four students shook hands with him, with the fine tolerance of young men intending much greater achievements than their teacher. They wouldn't speak on communicator again, because their messages might be picked up on Weald.

Of course, for this high heroic action to be successful, it had to be performed with the stealth of sneak-thieves.

What seemed a long time passed. The one ship turned slowly upon some unseen axis. It wavered back and forth, seeking a point of aim. A second twisted in its place. A third put on the barest trace of solar system drive to get clear of the rest. The fourth—

One ship vanished. It had gone into overdrive, heading for Dara at many times the speed of light. Another. Two more.

That was all. The remainder of the fleet hung clumsily in emptiness. And Calhoun worriedly went over in his mind the lessons he'd given in such a pathetically small number of days. If the four ships reached Dara, their pilots would be heroes. Calhoun had presented them with that estate over their bitter objection. But they would glory in it—if they reached Dara.

Maril looked at him with very strange eyes.

"Now what?" she asked.

"We hang around," said Calhoun, "to see if anybody comes up from Weald to find out what's happened. It's always possible to pick up a sort of signal when a ship goes into overdrive. Usually it doesn't mean a thing. Nobody pays any attention. But if somebody comes out here..."

"What?"

"It'll be regrettable," said Calhoun. He was suddenly very tired. "It'll spoil any chance of our coming back and stealing some more food, like interstellar mice. If they find out what we've done they'll expect us to try it again. They might get set to fight. Or they might simply land the rest of these ships."

"If I'd realized what you were about," said Maril, "I'd have joined in the lessons. I could have piloted a ship."

"You wouldn't have wanted to," said Calhoun. He yawned. "You wouldn't want to be a heroine. No normal girl does."

"Why?"

"Korvan," said Calhoun. He yawned again. "I've asked about him. He's been trying very desperately to deserve well of his fellow blueskins. All he's accomplished is develop a way to starve painlessly. He wouldn't feel comfortable with a girl who'd helped make starving unnecessary. He'd admire you politely, but he'd never marry you. And you know it."

She shook her head, but it was not easy to tell whether she denied the reaction of Korvan, whom Calhoun had never met, or denied that he was more important to her than anything else. The last was what Calhoun plainly implied.

"You don't seem to be trying to be a hero!" she protested.

"I'd enjoy it," admitted Calhoun, "but I have a job to do. It's got to be done. It's more important than being admired."

"You could take another ship back," she told him. "It would be worth more to Dara than the Med Ship is! And then everybody would realize that you'd planned everything."

"Ah," said Calhoun, "but you've no idea how much this ship matters to Dara!"

He seated himself at the controls. He slipped headphones over his ears. He listened. Very, very carefully, he monitored all the wave lengths and wave forms he could discover in use on Weald. There was no mention of the oddity of behavior of shiploads of surplus grain aloft. There was no mention of the ships at all. There was plenty of mention of Dara, and blueskins, and of the vicious political fight now going on to see which political party could promise the most complete protection against blueskins.

After a full hour of it, Calhoun flipped off his receptor and swung the Med Ship to an exact, painstakingly precise aim at the sun around which Dara rolled. He said, "Overdrive coming, Murgatroyd!"

Murgatroyd grabbed. The stars went out and the universe reeled and the Med Ship became a sort of cosmos all its own, into which no signal could come, no danger could enter, and in which there could be no sound except those minute ones made to prevent silence.

Calhoun yawned again.

"Now there's nothing to be done for a day or two," he said wearily, "and I'm beginning to understand why people sleep all they can, on Dara. It's one way not to feel hungry. And one dreams such delicious meals! But looking hungry is a social requirement, on Dara."

Maril said tensely, "You're going back? After they took the ship from you?"

"The job's not finished," he explained. "Not even the famine's ended, and the famine's a second-order effect. If there were no such thing as a blueskin, there'd be no famine. Food could be traded for. We've got to do something to make sure there are no more famines."

She looked at him oddly.

"It would be desirable," she said with irony. "But you can't do it."

"Not today, no," he admitted. Then he said longingly, "I didn't get much sleep on the way here, while running a seminar on astrogation. I think I'll take a nap."

She rose and almost ostentatiously went into the other cabin, to leave him alone. He shrugged. He settled down into the chair which, to let a Med Ship man break the monotony of life in unchanging surroundings, turned into a comfortable sleeping arrangement. He fell instantly asleep.

For very many ship-hours, then, there was no action or activity or happening of any imaginable consequence in the Med Ship. Very, very far away, light-years distant and light-years apart, four shiploads of grain hurtled toward the famine-stricken planet of blueskins. Each great ship had a single semiskilled blueskin for pilot and crew.

Thousands of millions of suns blazed with violence appropriate to their stellar types in a galaxy of which a very small proportion had been explored and colonized by humanity. The human race was now to be counted in quadrillions on scores of hundreds of inhabited worlds, but the tiny Med Ship seemed the least significant of all possible created things.

It could travel between star-systems and even star-clusters, but it was not yet capable of crossing the continent of suns on which the human race arose. And between any two solar systems the journeying of the Med Ship consumed much time. Which would be maddening for someone with no work to do or no resources in himself, or herself.

On the second ship-day Calhoun labored painstakingly and somewhat distastefully at the little biological laboratory. Maril watched him in a sort of brooding silence. Murgatroyd slept much of the time, with his furry tail wrapped meticulously across his nose.

Toward the end of the day Calhoun finished his task. He had a matter of six or seven cubic centimeters of clear liquid as the conclusion of a long process of culturing, and examination by microscope, and again culturing plus final filtration. He looked at a clock and calculated time.

"Better wait until tomorrow," he observed, and put the bit of clear liquid in a temperature-controlled place of safekeeping.

"What is it?" asked Maril. "What's it for?"

"It's part of a job I have on hand," said Calhoun. He considered. "How about some music?"

She looked astonished. But he set up an instrument and fed microtape into it and settled back to listen. Then there was music such as she had never heard before. It was another device to counteract isolation and monotonous between-planet voyages. To keep it from losing its effectiveness, Calhoun rationed himself on music, as on other things.

Any indulgence frequently repeated would become a habit, in the sense that it would give no special pleasure when indulged in, but would make for stress if it were omitted. Calhoun deliberately went for weeks between uses of his recordings, so that music was an event to be looked forward to and cherished.

When he tapered off the stirring symphonies of Kun Gee with tranquilizing, soothing melodies from the Rim School of composers, Maril regarded him with a very peculiar gaze indeed.

"I think I understand now," she said slowly, "why you don't act like other people. Toward me, for example. The way you live gives you what other people have to get in crazy ways—making their work feed their vanity, and justify pride, and make them feel significant. But you can put your whole mind on your work."

He thought it over.

"Med Ship routine is designed to keep one healthy in his mind," he admitted. "It works pretty well. It satisfies all my mental appetites. But there are instincts..."

She waited. He did not finish.

"What do you do about the instincts that work and music and such things can't satisfy?"

Calhoun grinned wryly, "I'm stern with them. I have to be."

He stood up and plainly expected her to go into the other cabin for the night. She went.

It was after breakfast time of the next ship-day when he got out the sample of clear liquid he'd worked so long to produce.

"We'll see how it works," he observed. "Murgatroyd's handy in case of a slip-up. It's perfectly safe so long as he's aboard and there are only the two of us."

She watched as he injected half a cc. under his own skin. Then she shivered a little.

"What will it do?"

"That remains to be seen." He paused a moment. "You and I," he said with some dryness, "make a perfect test for anything. If you catch something from me, it will be infectious indeed!"

She gazed at him utterly without comprehension.

He took his own temperature. He brought out the folios which were his orders, covering each of the planets he should give a standard Medical Service inspection. Weald was there. Dara wasn't. But a Med Service man has much freedom of action, even when only keeping up the routine of normal Med Service. When catching up on badly neglected operations, he necessarily has much more. Calhoun went over the folios.

Two hours later he took his temperature again. He looked pleased. He made an entry in the ship's log. Two hours later yet he found himself drinking thirstily and looked more pleased still.

He made another entry in the log and matter-of-factly drew a small quantity of blood from his own vein and called to Murgatroyd. Murgatroyd submitted amiably to the very trivial operation Calhoun carried out. Calhoun put away the equipment and saw Maril staring at him with a certain look of shock.

"It doesn't hurt him," Calhoun explained. "Right after he's born there's a tiny spot on his flank that has the pain-nerves desensitized. Murgatroyd's all right. That's what he's for!"

"But he's your friend!" said Maril.

Murgatroyd, despite his small size and furriness, had all the human attributes an animal which lives with humans soon acquires. Calhoun looked at him with affection.

"He's my assistant. I don't ask anything of him that I can do myself. But we're both Med Service. And I do things for him that he can't do for himself. For example, I make coffee for him."

Murgatroyd heard the familiar word. He said, "*Chee!*"

"Very well," agreed Calhoun. "We'll all have some."

He made coffee. Murgatroyd sipped at the cup especially made for his little paws. Once he scratched at the place on his flank which had no pain nerves. It itched. But he was perfectly content. Murgatroyd would always be contented when he was somewhere near Calhoun.

Another hour went by. Murgatroyd climbed up into Calhoun's lap and with a determined air went to sleep there. Calhoun disturbed him long enough to get an instrument out of his pocket. He listened to Murgatroyd's heartbeat, while Murgatroyd dozed.

"Maril," he said. "Write down something for me. The time, and ninety-six, and one-twenty over ninety-four."

She obeyed, not comprehending. Half an hour later, still not stirring to disturb Murgatroyd, he had her write down another time and sequence of figures, only slightly different from the first. Half an hour later still, a third set. But then he put Murgatroyd down, well satisfied.

He took his own temperature. He nodded.

"Murgatroyd and I have one more chore to do," he told her. "Would you go in the other cabin for a moment?"

Disturbed, she went into the other cabin. Calhoun drew a small sample of blood from the insensitive area on Murgatroyd's flank. Murgatroyd submitted with complete confidence in the man. In ten minutes Calhoun had diluted the sample, added an anticoagulant, shaken it up thoroughly, and filtered it to clarity with all red and white corpuscles removed. Another Med Ship man would have considered that Calhoun had had Murgatroyd prepare a splendid small sample of antibody-containing serum, in case something got out of hand. It would assuredly take care of two patients.

But a Med Ship man would also have known that it was simply one of those scrupulous precautions a Med Ship man takes when using cultures from store.

Calhoun put the sample away and called Maril back.

"It was nothing," he explained, "but you might have felt uncomfortable. We simply had a bit of Med Service routine that had to be gone through. It's all right now."

He offered no further explanation. She said, "I'll fix lunch." She hesitated. "You brought some food from the first Weald ship. Do you want to—"

He shook his head.

"I'm squeamish," he admitted. "The trouble on Dara is Med Service fault. Before my time, but still…I'll stick to rations until everybody eats."

He watched her unobtrusively as the day went on. Presently he considered that she was slightly flushed. Shortly after the evening meal of singularly unappetizing Darian rations, she drank thirstily. He did not comment. He brought out cards and showed her a complicated game of solitaire in which mental arithmetic and expert use of probability increased one's chance of winning.

By midnight she'd learned the game and played it absorbedly. Calhoun was able to scrutinize her without appearing to do so, and he was satisfied again. When he mentioned that the Med Ship should arrive off Dara in eight hours more, she put the cards away and went into the other cabin.

Calhoun wrote up the log. He added the notes that Maril had made for him, of Murgatroyd's pulse and blood pressure after the injection of the same culture that produced fever and thirstiness in himself and later, without contact with him or the culture, in Maril. He put a professional comment at the end:

The culture seems to have retained its normal characteristics during long storage in the spore state. It received and reproduced rapidly. I injected .5 cc. under my skin and in less than one hour my temperature was 30.8° C. An hour later it was 30.9° C. This was its peak. It immediately returned to normal. The only other observable symptom was slightly increased thirst. Bloodpressure and pulse remained normal. The other person in the Med Ship displayed the same symptoms, in prompt and complete repetition, without physical contact.

He went to sleep, with Murgatroyd curled up in his cubbyhole, his tail draped carefully over his nose.

The Med Ship broke out of overdrive at 1300 hours, ship-time. Calhoun made contact with the grid and was promptly lowered to the ground.

It was almost two hours later, at 1500 hours ship-time, when the people of Dara were informed by broadcast that Calhoun was to be executed immediately.

CHAPTER SEVEN

From the viewpoint of Darians, who were also blueskins, the decision of Calhoun's guilt and the decision to execute him were reasonable enough. Maril protested fiercely, and her testimony agreed with Calhoun's in every respect, but from a blueskin viewpoint their own statements were damning.

Calhoun had taken four young astrogators to space. They were the only semiskilled space pilots Dara had. There were no fully qualified men. Calhoun had asked for them, and taken them out to emptiness, and there he had instructed them in modern guidance methods for ships of space.

So far there was no disagreement. He'd proposed to make them more competent pilots; more capable of driving a ship to Orede, for example, to raid the enormous cattle herds there. And he'd had them drive the Med Ship to Weald, against which there could be no objection.

But just before arrival he had tricked all four of them by giving them drugged coffee. He'd destroyed the lethal bacterial cultures they'd been ordered to dump on Weald. Then he'd sent the four student pilots off separately, so he and Maril claimed, in huge ships crammed with grain. But those ships were not to be believed in, anyhow.

Nobody believed in shiploads of grain to be had for the taking. They did know that the only four partially experienced space pilots on Dara had been taken away and by Calhoun's own story sent out of the ship after they'd been drugged.

Had they been trained, and had they been helped or even permitted to sow the seeds of plague on Weald, and had they come back prepared to pass on training to other men to handle other space ships now feverishly being built in hidden places on Dara, then Dara might have a chance of survival.

But a space battle with only partly trained pilots would be hazardous at best. With no trained pilots at all, it would be hopeless. So Calhoun, by his own story, appeared to have doomed every living being on Dara to massacre from the bombs of Weald.

It was this last angle which destroyed any chance of anybody believing in such fairy-tale objects as ships loaded down with grain. Calhoun had shattered Dara's feeble hope of resistance. Weald had some ships and could build or buy others faster than Dara could hope to construct them.

Equally important, Weald had a plenitude of experienced spacemen to man some ships fully and train the crews of others. If it had become desperately busy fighting plague, then a fleet to exterminate life on Dara would be delayed. Dara might have gained time at least to build ships which could ram their enemies and destroy them that way.

But Calhoun had made it impossible. If he told the truth and Weald already had a fleet of huge ships which only needed to be emptied of grain and filled with guns and men, then Dara was doomed. But if he did not tell the truth it was equally doomed by his actions. So Calhoun would be killed.

His execution was to take place in the open space of the landing-grid, with vision cameras transmitting the sight over all the blueskin planet. Half-starved men with grisly blue blotches on their skins, marched him to the center of the largest level space on the planet which was not desperately being cultivated. Their hatred showed in their expressions. Bitterness and fury surrounded Calhoun like a wall. Most of Dara would have liked to have seen him killed in a manner as atrocious as his crime, but no conceivable death would be satisfying.

So the affair was coldly businesslike, with not even insults offered to him. He was left to stand alone in the very center of the landing-grid floor. There were a hundred blasters which would fire upon him at the same instant. He would not only be killed; he would be destroyed. He would be vaporized by the blue-white flames poured upon him.

His death was remarkably close, nothing remaining but the order to fire, when loudspeakers from the landing-grid office froze everything. One of the grain ships from Weald had broken out of overdrive and its pilot was triumphantly calling for landing coordinates. The grid office relayed his call to loudspeaker circuits as the quickest way to get it on the communication system of the whole planet.

"Calling ground," boomed the triumphant voice of the first of the student pilots Calhoun had trained. "Calling ground! Pilot Franz in captured ship requests coordinates for landing! Purpose of landing is to deliver half a million bushels of grain captured from the enemy!"

At first, nobody dared believe it. But the pilot could be seen on vision. He was known. No blueskin would be left alive long enough to be used as a decoy by the men of Weald! Presently the giant ship on its second voyage to Dara—the first had been a generation ago, when it threatened death and destruction—appeared as a dark pinpoint in the sky. It came down and down, and presently it hovered over the center of the tarmac, where Calhoun composedly stood on the spot where he was to have been executed.

The landing-grid crew shifted the ship to one side, and only then did Calhoun stroll in a leisurely fashion toward the Med Ship by the grid's metal-lace wall.

The big ship touched ground, and its exit port revolved and opened, and the student pilot stood there grinning and heaving out handfuls of grain. There was a swarming, yelling, deliriously triumphant crowd, then, where only minutes before there'd been a mob waiting to rejoice when Calhoun's living body exploded into flame.

They no longer hated Calhoun, but he had to fight his way to the Med Ship, nevertheless. He was surrounded by ecstatically admiring citizens of Dara. They shouted praise and rejoicing in his ears until he was half-deafened, and they almost tore his clothing from them in their desire to touch, to pat, to assure him of their gratitude and affection, minutes since they'd thirsted for his blood.

Two hours after the first ship, a second landed. Dara went wild again. Four hours later still, the third arrived. The fourth came down to ground on the following day.

When Calhoun faced the executive and cabinet of Dara for the second time his tone and manner were very dry.

"Now," he said curtly, "I would like a few more astrogators to train. I think it likely that we can raid the Wealdian grain fleet one more time, and in so doing get the beginning of a fleet for defense. I insist, however, that it must not be used in combat. We might as well be sensible about this situation! After all, four shiploads of grain won't break the famine! They'll help a lot, but they're only the beginning of what's needed for a planetary population!"

"How much grain can we hope for?" demanded a man with a blue mark covering all his chin.

Calhoun told him.

"How long before Weald can have a fleet overhead, dropping fusion bombs?" demanded another, grimly.

Calhoun named a time. But then he said, "I think we can keep them from dropping bombs if we can get the grain fleet and some capable astrogators."

"How?"

He told them. It was not possible to tell the whole story of what he considered sensible behavior. An emotional program can be presented and accepted immediately. A plan of action which is actually intelligent, considering all elements of a situation, has to be accepted piecemeal. Even so, the military men growled.

"We've plenty of heavy elements," said one. "If we'd used our brains, we'd have more bombs than Weald can hope for! We could turn that whole planet into a smoking cinder!"

"Which," said Calhoun acidly, "would give you some satisfaction but not an ounce of food! And food's more important than satisfaction. Now, I'm going to take off for Weald again. I'll want somebody to build an emergency device for my ship, and I'll want the four pilots I've trained and twenty more candidates. And I'd like to have some decent rations! The last trip brought back two million bushels of grain. You can certainly spare adequate food for twenty men for a few days!"

It took some time to get the special device constructed, but the Med Ship lifted in two days more. The device for which it had waited was simply a preventive of the disaster overtaking the ship from the mine on Orede. It was essentially a tank of liquid oxygen, packed in the space from which stores had been taken away. When the ship's air supply was pumped past it, first moisture and then CO_2 froze out.

Then the air flowed over the liquefied oxygen at a rate to replace the CO_2 with more useful breathing material. Then the moisture was restored to the air as it warmed again. For so long as the oxygen lasted, fresh air for any number of men could be kept purified and breathable. The Med Ship's normal equipment could take care of no more than ten. But with this it could journey to Weald with almost any complement on board.

Maril stayed on Dara when the Med Ship left. Murgatroyd protested shrilly when he discovered her about to be closed out by the closing airlock.

"*Chee!*" he said indignantly. "*Chee! Chee!*"

"No," said Calhoun. "We'll be crowded enough anyhow. We'll see her later."

He nodded to one of the first four student pilots, who crisply made contact with the landing-grid office, and very efficiently supervised as the grid took the ship up. The other three of the four first-trained men explained every move to sub-classes assigned to each. Calhoun moved about, listening and making certain that the instruction was up to standard.

He felt queer, acting as the supervisor of an educational institution in space. He did not like it. There were twenty-four men beside himself crowded into the Med Ship's small interior. They got in each other's way. They trampled on each other. There was always somebody eating, and always somebody sleeping, and there was no need whatever for the background tape to keep the ship from being intolerably quiet. But the air system worked well enough, except once when the reheating unit quit and the air inside the ship went down below freezing before the trouble could be found and corrected.

The journey to Weald, this time, took seven days because of the training program in effect. Calhoun bit his nails over the delay. But it was necessary for each of the students to make his own line-ups on Weald's sun, and compute distances, and for each of them to practise maneuverings that would presently be called for. Calhoun hoped desperately that preparations for active warfare did not move fast on Weald.

He believed, however, that in the absence of direct news from Dara, Wealdian officials would take the normal course of politicos. They had proclaimed the ship from Orede an attack from Dara. Therefore, they would specialize on defensive measures before plumping for offense. They'd get patrol ships out to spot invasion ships long before they worked on a fleet to destroy the blueskins. It would meet the public demand for defense.

Calhoun was right. The Med Ship made its final approach to Weald under Calhoun's own control. He'd made brightness-measurements on his previous journey and he used them again. They would not be strictly accurate, because a sunspot could knock all meaning out of any reading beyond two decimal places. But the first breakout was just far enough from the Wealdian system for Calhoun to be able to pick out its planets with the electron telescope at maximum magnification. He could aim for Weald itself, allowing, of course, for the lag in the apparent motion of its image because of the limited speed of light. He tried the briefest of overdrive hops, and came out within the solar system and well inside any watching patrol.

That was pure fortune. It continued. He'd broken through the screen of guard ships in undetectable overdrive. He was within half an hour's solar system drive of the grain fleet. There was no alarm, at first. Of course radars spotted the Med Ship as an object, but nobody paid attention. It was not headed for Weald. It was probably assumed to be a guard boat itself. Such mistakes do happen.

Again from the storage space from which supplies had been removed, Calhoun produced vacuum suits. The four first students went out, each escorting a less-accustomed neophyte and all fastened firmly together with space ropes. They warmed the interiors of four ships and went on to others. Presently there were eight ships making ready for an interstellar journey, each with a scared but resolute new pilot familiarizing himself with its controls. There were sixteen ships. Twenty. Twenty-three.

A guard ship came humming out from Weald. It would be armed, of course. It came droning, droning up the forty-odd thousand miles from the planet. Calhoun swore. He could not call his students and tell them what was toward. The guard ship would overhear. He could not trust untried young men to act rationally if they were unaware and the guard ship arrived and matter-of-factly attempted to board one of them.

Then he was inspired. He called Murgatroyd, placed him before the communicator, and set it at voice-only transmission. This was familiar enough, to Murgatroyd. He'd often seen Calhoun use a communicator.

"*Chee!*" shrilled Murgatroyd. "*Chee-chee!*"

A startled voice came out of the speaker: "What's that?"

"*Chee*," said Murgatroyd zestfully.

The communicator was talking to him. Murgatroyd adored three things, in order. One was Calhoun. The second was coffee. The third was pretending to converse like a human being. The speaker said explosively, "You there, identify yourself!"

"*Chee-chee-chee-chee!*" observed Murgatroyd. He wriggled with pleasure and added, reasonably enough, "*Chee!*"

The communicator bawled, "Calling ground! Calling ground! Listen to this! Something that ain't human's talking at me on a communicator! Listen in an' tell me what to do!"

Murgatroyd interposed with another shrill, "*Chee!*"

Then Calhoun pulled the Med Ship slowly away from the clump of still-lifeless grain ships. It was highly improbable that the guard boat would carry an electron telescope. Most likely it would have only an echo-radar, and so could determine only that an object of some sort moved of its own accord in space. Calhoun let the Med Ship accelerate. That would be final evidence. The grain ships were between Weald and its sun. Even electron telescopes on the ground—and electron telescopes were ultimately optical telescopes with electronic amplification—could not get a good image of the ship through sunlit atmosphere.

"*Chee?*" asked Murgatroyd solicitously. "*Chee-chee-chee?*"

"Is it blueskins?" shakily demanded the voice from the guard boat. "Ground! Ground! Is it blueskins?"

A heavy, authoritative voice came in with much greater volume. "That's no human voice," it said harshly. "Approach its ship and send back an image. Don't fire first unless it heads for ground."

The guard ship swerved and headed for the Med Ship. It was still a very long way off.

"*Chee-chee,*" said Murgatroyd encouragingly.

Calhoun changed the Med Ship's course. The guard ship changed course too. Calhoun let it draw nearer, but only a little. He led it away from the fleet of grain ships.

He swung his electron telescope on them. He saw a spacesuited figure outside one, safely roped, however. It was easy to guess that someone had meant to return to the Med Ship for orders or to make a report, and found the Med Ship gone. He'd go back inside and turn on a communicator.

"*Chee!*" said Murgatroyd.

The heavy voice boomed. "You there! This is a human-occupied world! If you come in peace, cut your drive and let our guard ship approach!"

Murgatroyd replied in an interested but doubtful tone. The booming voice bellowed. Another voice of higher authority took over. Murgatroyd was entranced that so many people wanted to talk to him. He made what for him was practically an oration. The last voice spoke persuasively and suavely.

"*Chee-chee-chee-chee,*" said Murgatroyd.

One of the grain ships flickered and ceased to be. It had gone into overdrive. Another. And another. Suddenly they began to flick out of sight by twos and threes.

"*Chee,*" said Murgatroyd with a note of finality.

The last grain ship vanished.

"Calling guard ship," said Calhoun dryly. "This is Med Ship *Aesclipus Twenty*. I called here a couple of weeks ago. You've been talking to my *tormal*, Murgatroyd."

A pause. A blank pause. Then profanity of deep and savage intemperance.

"I've been on Dara," said Calhoun.

Dead silence fell.

"There's a famine there," said Calhoun deliberately. "So the grain ships you've had in orbit have been taken away by men from Dara—blueskins if you like—to feed themselves and their families. They've been dying of hunger and they don't like it."

There was a single burst of the unprintable. Then the formerly suave voice said waspishly, "Well? The Med Service will hear of your interference!"

"Yes," said Calhoun. "I'll report it myself. I have a message for you. Dara is ready to pay for every ounce of grain and for the ships it was stored in. They'll pay in heavy metals—irridium, uranium, that sort of thing."

The suave voice fairly curdled.

"As if we'd allow anything that was ever on Dara to touch ground here!"

"Ah! But there can be sterilization. To begin with metals, uranium melts at 1150° centigrade, and tungsten at 3370° and irridium at 2350°. You could load such things and melt them down in space and then tow them home. And you can actually sterilize a lot of other useful materials!"

The suave voice was infuriated: "I'll report this! You'll suffer for this!"

Calhoun said pleasantly, "I'm sure that what I say is being recorded, so that I'll add that it's perfectly practical for Wealdians to land on Dara, take whatever property they think wise—to pay for damage done by blueskins, of course—and get back to Wealdian ships with absolutely no danger of carrying contagion. If you'll make sure the recording's clear..."

He described, clearly and specifically, exactly how a man could be outfitted to walk into any area of any conceivable contagion, do whatever seemed necessary in the way of looting—but Calhoun did not use the word—and then return to his fellows with no risk whatever of bringing back infection. He gave exact details.

Then he said, "My radar says you've four ships converging on me to blast me out of space. I sign off."

The Med Ship disappeared from normal space, and entered that improbably stressed area of extension which it formed about itself and in which physical constants were wildly strange. For one thing, the speed of light in overdrive-stressed space had not been measured yet. It was too high. For another, a ship could travel very many times 186,000 miles per second in overdrive.

The Med Ship did just that. There was nobody but Calhoun and Murgatroyd on board. There was companionable silence, with only the small threshold-of-perception sounds which one did not often notice.

Calhoun luxuriated in regained privacy. For seven days he'd had twenty-four other human beings crowded into the two cabins of the ship, with never so much as one yard of space between himself and someone else. One need not be snobbish to wish to be alone sometimes!

Murgatroyd licked his whiskers thoughtfully.

"I hope," said Calhoun, "that things work out right. But they may remember on Dara that I'm responsible for some ten million bushels of grain reaching them. Maybe, just possibly, they'll listen to me and act sensibly. After all, there's only one way to break a famine. Not with ten million bushels for a whole planet! And certainly not with bombs!"

Driving direct, without pausing for practising, the Med Ship could arrive at Dara in a little more than five days. Calhoun looked forward to relaxation. As a beginning he made ready to give himself an adequate meal for the first time since first landing on Dara. Then, presently, he sat down to a double meal of Darian famine-rations, which were far from appetizing. But there wasn't anything else on board.

He had some pleasure later, though, envisioning what went on in the normal, non-overdrive universe. Suns flared, and comets hurtled on their way, and clouds formed and dropped down rain, and all sorts of celestial and meteorological phenomena took place. On Weald, obviously, there would be purest panic.

The vanishing of the grain fleet wouldn't be charged against twenty-four men. A Darian fleet would be suspected, and with the suspicion would come terror, and with terror a governmental crisis. Then there'd be a frantic seizure of any craft that could take to space, and the agitated improvisation of a space fleet.

But besides that, biological-warfare technicians would examine Calhoun's instructions for equipment by which armed men could be landed on a plague-stricken planet and then safely taken off again. Military and governmental officials would come to the eminently sane conclusion that while Calhoun could not well take active measures against blueskins, as a sane and proper citizen of the galaxy he would be on the side of law and order and propriety and justice—in short, of Weald. So they ordered sample anticontagion suits made according to Calhoun's directions, and they had them tested. They worked admirably.

On Dara, while Calhoun journeyed placidly back to it, grain was distributed lavishly, and everybody on the planet had their cereal ration almost doubled. It was still not a comfortable ration, but the relief was great. There was considerable gratitude felt for Calhoun, which as usual included a lively anticipation of further favors to come. Maril was interviewed repeatedly, as the person best able to discuss him, and she did his reputation no harm. That was all that happened on Dara…

No. There was something else. A very curious thing, too. There was a spread of mild symptoms which nobody could exactly call a disease. They lasted only a few hours. A person felt slightly feverish, and ran a temperature which peaked at 30.9° centigrade, and drank more water than usual. Then his temperature went back to normal and he forgot all about it. There have always been such trivial epidemics. They are rarely recorded, because few people think to go to a doctor. That was the case here.

Calhoun looked ahead a little, too. Presently the fleet of grain ships would arrive and unload and lift again for Orede, and this time they would make an infinity of slaughter among wild cattle herds, and bring back incredible quantities of fresh-slaughtered frozen beef. Almost everybody would get to taste meat again, which would be most gratifying.

Then, the industries of Dara would labor at government-required tasks. An astonishing amount of fissionable material would be fashioned into bombs—a concession by Calhoun—and plastic factories would make an astonishing number of plastic sag-suits. And large shipments of heavy metals in ingots would be made to the planet's capital city and there would be some guns and minor items.

Perhaps somebody could have predicted any of these items in advance, but it was unlikely that anyone did. Nobody but Calhoun, however, would ever have put them together and hoped very urgently that things would work out. He could see a promising total result. In fact, in the

Med Ship hurtling through space, on the fourth day of his journey, he thought of an improvement that could be made in the sum of all those happenings when they got mixed together.

He got back to Dara. Maril came to the Med Ship. Murgatroyd greeted her with enthusiasm.

"Something strange has happened," said Maril, very much subdued. "I told you that sometimes blueskin markings fade out on children, and then neither they nor their children ever have markings again."

"Yes," said Calhoun. "I remember that you told me."

"And you were reminded of a group of viruses on Tralee. You said they only took hold of people in terribly bad physical condition, but then they could be passed on from mother to child, until sometimes they died out."

Calhoun blinked.

"Yes?"

"Korvan," said Maril very carefully. "Has worked out an idea that that's what happens to the blueskin markings on Darians. He thinks that people almost dead of the plague could get the virus, and if they recovered from the plague pass the virus on and be blueskins."

"Interesting," said Calhoun, noncommittally.

"And when we went to Weald," said Maril very carefully indeed, "you were working with some culture material. You wrote quite a lot about it in the ship's log. You gave yourself an injection. Remember? And Murgatroyd? You wrote down your temperature, and Murgatroyd's?" She moistened her lips. "You said that if infection passed between us, something would be very infectious indeed?"

"This is a long discussion," said Calhoun. "Does it arrive at a point?"

"It does," said Maril. "Thousands of people are having their pigment-spots fade away. Not only children but grownups. And Korvan has found out that it always seems to happen after a day when they felt feverish and very thirsty, and then felt all right again. You tried out something that made you feverish and thirsty. I had it too, in the ship. Korvan thinks there's been an epidemic of something that is obliterating the blue spots on everybody that catches it. There are always trivial epidemics that nobody notices. Korvan's found evidence of one that's making *blueskin* no longer a word with any meaning."

"Remarkable!" said Calhoun.

"Did you do it?" asked Maril. "Did you start a harmless epidemic that wipes out the virus that makes blueskins?"

Calhoun said in feigned astonishment, "How can you think such a thing, Maril?"

"Because I was there," said Maril. She said, somehow desperately, "I know you did it! But the question is, are you going to tell? When people find they're not blueskins any longer, when there's no such thing as a blueskin any longer, will you tell them why?"

"Naturally not," said Calhoun. "Why?" Then he guessed. "Has Korvan—"

"He thinks," said Maril, "that he thought it up all by himself. He's found the proof. He's very proud. I'd have to tell him how the ideas got into his head if you were going to tell. And he'd be ashamed and angry."

Calhoun considered, staring at her.

"How it happened doesn't matter," he said at last. "The idea of anybody doing it deliberately would be disturbing, too. It shouldn't get about. So it seems much the best thing for Korvan to discover what's happened to the blueskin pigment, and how it happened. But not why."

She read his face carefully.

"You aren't doing it as a favor to me," she decided. "You'd rather it was that way."

She looked at him for a long time, until he squirmed. Then she nodded and went away.

An hour later the Wealdian space fleet was reported massed in space and driving for Dara.

CHAPTER EIGHT

There were small scout ships which came on ahead of the main fleet. They'd originally been guard boats, intended for solar system duty only and quite incapable of overdrive. They'd come from Weald in the cargo holds of the liners now transformed into fighting ships. The scouts swept low, transmitting fine-screen images back to the fleet, of all they might see before they were shot down. They found the landing-grid. It contained nothing larger than Calhoun's Med Ship, *Aesclipus Twenty*.

They searched here and there. They flittered to and fro, scanning wide bands of the surface of Dara. The planet's cities and highways and industrial centers were wholly open to inspection from the sky. It looked as if the scouts hunted most busily for the fleet of former grain ships which Calhoun had said the blueskins had seized and rushed away. If the scouts looked for them, they did not find them.

Dara offered no opposition to the ships. Nothing rose to space to oppose or to resist their search. They went darting over every portion of the hungry planet, land and seas alike, and there was no sign of military preparedness against their coming. The huge ships of the main fleet waited while the scouts reported monotonously that they saw no sign of the stolen fleet. But the stolen fleet was the only means by which the planet could be defended. There could be no point in a pitched battle in emptiness. But a fleet with a planet to back it might be dangerous.

Hours passed. The Wealdian main fleet waited. There was no offensive movement by the fleet. There was no defensive action from the ground. With fusion-bombs certain to be involved in any actual conflict, there was something like an embarrassed pause. The Wealdian ships were ready to bomb. They were less anxious to be vaporized by possible suicide dashes of defending ships which might blow themselves up near contact with their enemies.

But a fleet cannot travel some light-years through space to make a mere threat. And the Wealdian fleet was furnished with the material for total devastation. It could drop bombs from hundreds, or thousands, or even tens of thousands of miles away. It could cover the world of Dara with mushroom clouds springing up and spreading to make a continuous pall of atomic-fusion products. And they could settle down and kill every living thing not destroyed by the explosions themselves. Even the creatures of the deepest oceans would die of deadly, purposely-contrived fallout particles.

The Wealdian fleet contemplated its own destructiveness. It found no capacity for defense on Dara. It moved forward.

But then a message went out from the capital city of Dara. It said that a ship in overdrive had carried word to a Darian fleet in space. The Darian fleet now hurtled toward Weald. It was a fleet of thirty-seven giant ships. They carried such-and-such bombs in such-and-such quantities. Unless its orders were countermanded, it would deliver those bombs on Weald, set to explode. If Weald bombed Dara, the orders could not be withdrawn. So Weald could bomb Dara. It could destroy all life on the pariah planet. But Weald would die with it.

The fleet ceased its advance. The situation was a stalemate with pure desperation on one side and pure frustration on the other. This was no way to end the war. Neither planet could trust the other, even for minutes. If they did not destroy each other simultaneously, as now was possible, each would expect the other to launch an unwarned attack at some other moment. Ultimately one or the other must perish, and the survivor would be the one most skilled in treachery.

But then the pariah planet made a new proposal. It would send a messenger ship to stop its own fleet's bombardment if Weald would accept payment of the grain ships and their cargos. It would pay in ingots of irridium and uranium and tungsten, and gold if Weald wished it, for all damages Weald might claim.

It would even pay indemnity for the miners of Orede, who had died by accident but perhaps in some sense through its fault. It would pay. But if it were bombed, Weald must spout atomic fire and the fleet of Weald would have no home planet to return to.

This proposal seemed both craven and foolish. It would allow the fleet of Weald to loot and then betray Dara. But it was Calhoun's idea. It seemed plausible to the admirals of Weald. They felt only contempt for blueskins. Contemptuously, they accepted the semi-surrender.

The broadcast waves of Dara told of agreement, and wild and fierce resentment filled the pariah planet's people. There was almost revolution to insist upon resistance, however hopeless and however fatal. But not all of Dara realized that a vital change had come about in the state of things on Dara. The enemy fleet had not a hint of it.

In menacing array, the invading fleet spread itself about the skies of Dara, well beyond the atmosphere. Harsh voices talked with increasing arrogance to the landing-grid staff. A monster ship of Weald came heavily down, riding the landing-grid's force-fields. It touched gently. Its occupants were apprehensive, but hungry for the loot they had been assured was theirs. The ship's outer hull would be sterilized before it returned to Weald, of course. And there was adequate protection for the landing-party.

Men came out of the ship's ports. They wore the double, transparent sag-suits Calhoun had suggested, which had been painstakingly tested, and which were perfect protection against contagion. They were double garments of plastic, with air tanks inside the inner flexible envelope.

Men wearing such sag-suits could walk about on Dara. They could work on Dara. They could loot with impunity and all contamination must remain outside the suits, and on their return to their ships they would simply stand in the airlocks while corrosive gases swirled around them, killing any possible organism of disease. Then, for extra assurance, when air from Weald filled the airlock again, the men would burn the outer plastic covering and step into the ship without ever having come within two layers of plastic of infection.

What loot they gathered, obviously, could be decontaminated before it was returned to Weald. Metals could be melted, if necessary. Gems could be sterilized. It was a most satisfactory discovery, to realize that blueskins could be not only scorned but robbed. There was only one bit of irrelevant information the space fleet of Weald did not have.

That information was that the people of Dara weren't blueskins any longer. There'd been a trivial epidemic...

The sag-suited men of Weald went zestfully about their business. They took over the landing-grid's operation, driving the Darian operators away. For the first time in history the operators of a landing-grid wore make-up to look like they did have blue pigment in their skins. They didn't. The Wealdian landing-party tested the grid's operation. They brought down another giant ship. Then another. And another.

Parties in the shiny sag-suits spread through the city. There were the huge stockpiles of precious metals, brought in readiness to be surrendered and carried away. Some men set to work to load these into the holds of the ships of Weald. Some went forthrightly after personal loot.

They came upon very few Darians. Those they saw kept sullenly away from them. They entered shops and took what they fancied. They zestfully removed the treasure of banks.

Triumphant and scornful reports went up to the hovering great ships. The blueskins, said the reports, were spiritless and cowardly. They permitted themselves to be robbed. They kept out of the way. It had been observed that the population was streaming out of the city, fleeing because they feared the ships' landing-parties. The blueskins had abjectly produced all they'd promised of precious metals, but there was more to be taken.

More ships came down, and more. Some of the first, heavily loaded, were lifted to emptiness again and the process of decontamination of their hulls began. There was jealousy among the ships in space for those upon the ground. The first-landed ships had had their choice of loot. There were squabblings about priorities, now that the navy of Weald plainly had a license to steal. There was confusion among the members of the landing-parties.

Discipline disappeared. Men in plastic sag-suits roved about as individuals, seeking what they might loot.

There were armed and alerted landing-parties around the grid itself, of course, but the capital city of Dara lay open. Men coming back with loot found their ships already lifted off to make room for others. They were pushed into re-embarking-parties of other ships. There were more and more men to be found on ships where they did not belong, and more and more not to be found where they did.

By the time half the fleet had been aground, there was no longer any pretense of holding a ship down until all its crew returned. There were too many other ships' companies clamoring for their turn to loot. The rosters of many ships, indeed, bore no particular relationship to the men actually on board.

There were less than fifteen ships whose to-be-fumigated holds were still emptied, when the watchful government of Dara broadcast a new message to the invaders. It requested that the looting stop. No matter what payment Weald claimed, it had taken payment five times over. Now was time to stop.

It was amusing. The space admiral of Weald ordered his ships alerted for action. The message ship, ordering the Darian fleet away from Weald, had been sent off long since. No other ship could get away now! The Darians could take their choice: accept the consequences of surrender, or the fleet would rise to throw down bombs.

Calhoun was asking politely to be taken to the Wealdian admiral when the trouble began. It wasn't on the ground, at all. Everything was under splendid control where a landing force occupied the grid and all the ground immediately about it. The space admiral had headquarters in the landing-grid office. Reports came in, orders were issued, admirably crisp salutes were exchanged among sag-suited men. Everything was in perfect shape there.

But there was panic among the ships in space. Communicators gave off horrified, panic-stricken yells. There were screamings. Intelligible communications ceased. Ships plunged crazily this way and that. Some vanished in overdrive. At least one plunged at full power into a Darian ocean.

The space admiral found himself in command of fifteen ships only out of all his former force. The rest of the fleet went through a period of hysterical madness. In some ships it lasted for minutes only. In others it went on for half an hour or more. Then they hung overhead, but did not reply to calls.

Calhoun arrived at the spaceport with Murgatroyd riding on his shoulder. A bewildered officer in a sag-suit halted him.

"I've come," said Calhoun, "to speak to the admiral. My name is Calhoun and I'm Med Service, and I think I met the admiral at a banquet a few weeks ago. He'll remember me."

"You'll have to wait," protested the officer. "There's some trouble—"

"Yes," said Calhoun. "I know about it. I helped design it. I want to explain it to the admiral. He needs to know what's happened, if he's to take appropriate measures."

There were jitterings. Many men in sag-suits had still no idea that anything had gone wrong. Some appeared, brightly carrying loot. Some hung eagerly around the airlocks of ships on the grid tarmac, waiting their turns to stand in corrosive gases for the decontamination of their suits, when they would burn the outer layers and step, aseptic and happy, into a Wealdian ship again. There they could think how rich they were going to be back on Weald.

But the situation aloft was bewildering and very, very ominous. There was strident argument. Presently Calhoun stood before the Wealdian admiral.

"I came to explain something," said Calhoun pleasantly. "The situation has changed. You've noticed it, I'm sure."

The admiral glared at him through two layers of plastic, which covered him almost like a gift-wrapped parcel.

"Be quick!" he rasped.

"First," said Calhoun, "there are no more blueskins. An epidemic of something or other has made the blue patches on the skins of Darians fade out. There have always been some who didn't have blue patches. Now nobody has them."

"Nonsense!" rasped the admiral. "And what has that got to do with this situation?"

"Why, everything," said Calhoun mildly. "It seems that Darians can pass for Wealdians whenever they please. That they *are* passing for Wealdians. That they've been mixing with your men, wearing sag-suits exactly like the one you're wearing now. They've been going aboard your ships in the confusion of returning looters. There's not a ship now aloft, which has been aground today, which hasn't from one to fifteen Darians—no longer blueskins— on board."

The admiral roared. Then his face turned gray.

"You can't take your fleet back to Weald," said Calhoun gently, "if you believe its crews have been exposed to carriers of the Dara plague. You wouldn't be allowed to land, anyhow."

The admiral said through stiff lips, "I'll blast—"

"No," said Calhoun, again gently. "When you ordered all ships alerted for action, the Darians on each ship released panic gas. They only needed tiny, pocket-sized containers of the gas for the job. They had them. They only needed to use air tanks from their sag-suits to protect themselves against the gas. They kept them handy.

"On nearly all your ships aloft your crews are crazy from panic gas. They'll stay that way until the air is changed. Darians have barricaded themselves in the control rooms of most if not all your ships. You haven't got a fleet. The few ships who will obey your orders—if they drop one bomb, our fleet off Weald will drop fifty.

"I don't think you'd better order offensive action. Instead, I think you'd better have your fleet medical officers come and learn some of the facts of life. There's no need for war between Dara and Weald, but if you insist…"

The admiral made a choking noise. He could have ordered Calhoun killed, but there was a certain appalling fact. The men aground from the fleet were breathing Wealdian air from tanks. It would last so long only. If they were taken on board the still obedient ships overhead, Darians would unquestionably be mixed with them. There was no way to take off the parties now aground without exposing them to contact with Darians, on the ground or in the ships. There was no way to sort out the Darians.

"I—I will give the orders," said the admiral thickly. "I do not know what you devils plan, but—I do not know how to stop you."

"All that's necessary," said Calhoun warmly, "is an open mind. There's a misunderstanding to be cleared up, and some principles of planetary health practises to be explained, and a certain amount of prejudice that has to be thrown away. But nobody need die of changing their minds. The Interstellar Medical Service has proved that over and over!"

Murgatroyd, perched on his shoulder, felt that it was time to take part in the conversation. He said, "*Chee-chee!*"

"Yes," agreed Calhoun. "We do want to get the job done. We're behind schedule now."

It was not, of course, possible for Calhoun to leave immediately. He had to preside at various meetings of the medical officers of the fleet and the health officials of Dara. He had to make explanations, and correct misapprehensions, and delicately suggest such biological experiments as would prove to the doctors of Weald that there was no longer a plague on Dara, whatever had been the case three generations before.

He had to sit by while an extremely self-confident young Darian doctor—one of his names was Korvan—rather condescendingly demonstrated that the former blue pigmentation was a viral product quite unconnected with the plague, and that it had been wiped out by a very trivial epidemic of such and such.

Calhoun regarded that young man with a detached interest. Maril thought him wonderful, even if she had to give him the material for his work. He agreed with her that he was wonderful. Calhoun shrugged and went on with his own work.

The return of loot, mutual, full, and complete agreement that Darians were no longer carriers of plague, if they had ever been—unless Weald convinced other worlds of this, Weald itself would join Dara in isolation from neighboring worlds. A messenger ship had to recall the twenty-seven ships once floating in orbit about Weald. Most of them would be used for some time, to bring beef from Orede.

Some would haul more grain from Weald. It would be paid for. There would be a need for commercial missions to be exchanged between Weald and Dara. There would have to be...

It was a full week before he could go to the little Med Ship and prepare for departure. Even then there were matters to be attended to. All the food-supplies that had been removed could not be replaced. There were biological samples to be replaced and some to be destroyed.

Maril came to the Med Ship again when he was almost ready to leave. She did not seem comfortable.

"I wanted you to meet Korvan," she said regretfully.

"I met him," said Calhoun. "I think he will be a most prominent citizen, in time. He has all the talents for it."

Maril smiled very faintly.

"But you don't admire him."

"I wouldn't say that," protested Calhoun. "After all, he is desirable to you, which is something I couldn't manage."

"You didn't try," said Maril. "Just as I didn't try to be fascinating to you. Why?"

Calhoun spread out his hands. But he looked at Maril with respect. Not every woman could have faced the fact that a man did not feel impelled to make passes at her. It is simply a fact that has nothing to do with desirability or charm or anything else.

"You're going to marry him," he said. "I hope you'll be very happy."

"He's the man I want," said Maril frankly. "And I doubt he'll ever look at another woman. He looks forward to splendid discoveries. I wish he didn't."

Calhoun did not ask the obvious question. Instead, he said thoughtfully, "There's something you could do. It needs to be done. The Med Service in this sector has been badly handled. There are a number of discoveries that need to be made. I don't think your Korvan would relish having things handed to him on a visible silver platter. But they should be known…"

Maril said, "I can guess what you mean. I dropped hints about the way the blueskin markings went away, yes. You've got books for me?"

Calhoun nodded. He found them.

"If we had only fallen in love with each other, Maril, we'd be a team! Too bad! These are a wedding present you'll do well to hide."

She put her hands in his.

"I like you almost as much as I like Murgatroyd! Yes! Korvan will never know, and he'll be a great man." Then she added defensively, "But I don't think he'll only discover things from hints I drop him. He'll make wonderful discoveries."

"Of which," said Calhoun, "the most remarkable is you. Good luck, Maril!"

She went away smiling. But she wiped her eyes when she was out of the ship.

Presently the Med Ship lifted. Calhoun aimed it for the next planet on the list of those he was to visit. After this one more he'd return to sector headquarters with a biting report to make on the way things had been handled before him.

"Overdrive coming, Murgatroyd!"

Then the stars went out and there was silence, and privacy, and a faint, faint, almost unbearable series of background sounds which kept the Med Ship from being totally unendurable.

Long, long days later the ship broke out of overdrive and Calhoun guided it to a round and sunlit world. In due time he thumbed the communicator button.

"Calling ground," he said crisply. "Calling ground! Med Ship *Aesclipus Twenty* reporting arrival and asking coordinates for landing. Purpose of landing is planetary health inspection. Our mass is fifty standard tons."

There was a pause while the beamed message went many, many thousands of miles. Then the speaker said, "*Aesclipus Twenty*, repeat your identification!"

Calhoun repeated it patiently. Murgatroyd watched with bright eyes. Perhaps he hoped to be allowed to have another long conversation with somebody by communicator.

"You are warned," said the communicator sternly, "that any deceit or deception about your identity or purpose in landing will be severely punished. We take few chances, here! If you wish to land notwithstanding this warning—"

"I'm coming in," said Calhoun. "Give me the coordinates."

He wrote them down. His expression was slightly pained. The Med Ship drove on, in solar system drive. Murgatroyd said, "*Chee-chee? Chee?*"

Calhoun sighed.

"That's right, Murgatroyd! Here we go again!"

THE END